# THE LAST FULL
# MEASURE

# THE LAST FULL
# MEASURE

# JACK CAMPBELL

SUBTERRANEAN PRESS ★ 2013

**First Edition**

**ISBN**
978-1-59606-568-0

**Ebook ISBN**
978-1-59606-569-7

Subterranean Press
PO Box 190106
Burton, MI 48519

**www.subterraneanpress.com**

**"THE NEXT PRISONER** is Mr. Abraham Lincoln, of Illinois."

Professor Joshua Chamberlain turned his head with careful movements so as not to excite the soldiers holding weapons at the back of the small, windowless courtroom. He sat on the end of a bench along with others arrested for offenses against national security, watching as a tall, gangly and rather unattractive man on the other end of the bench rose up like an ungainly stork coming to its feet.

The bailiff, a sergeant, faced the row of hooded military officers sitting at the front of the courtroom. "The prisoner awaits sentencing."

Before the judges could speak, Mr. Lincoln did. "The prisoner would greatly appreciate being told the charges against him."

After a pause, one of the judges spoke, his voice muffled by the hood he wore to conceal his identity. "You are charged with being a threat to the security of the United States of America. You have stirred up opposition to the government, you have encouraged those who would weaken and destroy us, and you have sought to undermine the strength of this great nation. I assume you will not dare to deny those charges?"

"I am to be given the opportunity to plead?" Lincoln said, speaking lightly despite the stern tone of the judge and despite the guards focusing their attention on him. "That is one of the precepts upon which this nation was founded, is it not? As is the right to a fair trial. As is life, liberty, and the pursuit of happiness. Have any of you, by chance, heard of this thing called liberty?"

"Do not presume to ask us questions! Do you have no answer for the charges against you?"

Lincoln shrugged with an unassuming manner, as if he were in a normal courtroom and addressing a jury of his peers. "You are like the man who planted a crop of wheat and then demanded to know why corn had not grown in his fields. You blame me for opposition to the government? Look no further than yourselves. These are *your* actions, and as the good book says, as ye sow so shall ye reap. You blame my words for the weaknesses that strike at the very foundation of our people? I did not create those weaknesses. Neither did you, but your acts perpetuate them. The monstrous injustice of slavery gnaws at the timbers of our Republic, not only in the South but also the North and the West. Our entire house trembles because slavery makes slaves of all who labor, and a small group of men enjoys a large proportion of the fruits."

Another judge spoke, his voice harsh. "We are the most free and most happy country this world has ever known. We are free because our strength and our vigilance keep us free."

Lincoln shook his head slowly and sorrowfully. "Gentlemen, you seem to believe that you are our strength, that our liberty is guarded by frowning battlements. Our reliance is not in such things. It is in our love of liberty. A liberty that you, sir, have placed in chains such as those that I and these other unfortunates now wear."

Chamberlain listened in amazement, moved by Lincoln's words despite his own fears of what fate the tribunal might soon assign Chamberlain himself. *I have never heard the issues set forth so plainly, even though the plight of the indentured factory workers of the North creates ever more unrest even in states which are technically free of slavery.*

"You see!" the second judge insisted to his comrades, pointing an accusing finger at the tall, ungraceful figure of Lincoln. "This is how he arouses the masses! This is why the northern states threaten rebellion and revolt! This is why the southern states must deal with agitators attempting to incite the slaves against their moral and proper state of benevolent servitude!"

Lincoln smiled, but this time his voice held a sharp edge. "If you wish to argue the virtues of slavery, perhaps you would care to have it tried on you personally?"

"I have heard enough. Death?" the third judge asked.

"Not until he and his words are forgotten! We don't need any more martyrs!"

"Rendition to Fortress Monroe," the first judge said. "The *Merrimac* is leaving for Hampton Roads tomorrow with other prisoners. They will have plenty of room for this Lincoln."

"Indefinite detention," the second judge added. "To be kept solitary so that he might no longer communicate to others his lies about the motives and wisdom of our founders."

A wise man would have sat silently as Lincoln was taken from the courtroom. Chamberlain knew that. Only by staying silent would Chamberlain have a chance to avoid drawing too much attention to himself in a place where the hooded officers served as judge and jury. But perhaps it was asking too much of a professor of rhetoric to remain silent under such circumstances, after having heard such words.

Chamberlain stood up, a strange crawling sensation arising between his shoulders as he heard a sound behind him and imagined a rifle barrel aimed at his back. "Our greatest founder, George Washington, would never have approved of this. I have read his papers."

The first judge halted a motion toward the bailiff aimed at silencing the prisoner and instead gazed at Chamberlain. "How did you gain access to the papers of the First President and Founder?"

"Is it not more important what I read there? That Washington did not become president as our histories read because he was installed by the military and the great land owners. He was instead elected by popular vote. So was John Adams and so was Jefferson!"

The second judge sounded amused. "And Jefferson's Co-President? Aaron Burr? Are you claiming that he was elected by popular vote as well?"

Chamberlain swallowed, his throat dry at the taunting tone of the judge. They were playing with him, letting his own words condemn him. Well, so be it. The tribunals convicted all who came before them so any hope of release had always been illusory. "Burr was elected *Vice*-President. It was the price for that, for demanding the authority to deal with a military officer corps packed with Federalist party supporters by President Adams, that led to this. Burr dismissed every Federalist from the officer ranks, replacing them with Democratic Republican loyalists, and every administration after followed the example not of Washington but of Adams and Burr. That is what turned our Republic into a sham. The military of the United States has become a tool and an instrument of partisan politics. It does not serve the people, it serves those whose power and wealth control the government."

"We are free," the first judge said. "Free because those who would defame our history and the motives of those who protect us are punished for their crimes. Forty years agricultural service," he finished.

Forty years on one of the plantations, laboring in conditions at least as bad as those suffered by the negro slaves. His odds of surviving the sentence were very small, but that was the intent of the judges.

Chamberlain was grabbed by one of the guards and marched out along with Lincoln. The two men stood side by side for a moment as their guards received orders, the tall man from Illinois gazing somberly down the hallway. "Thank you for your courage, sir," Lincoln said in a soft voice. "I do not know what our lot may be, whether destruction or a rebirth of liberty. But whatever our fate, we must ourselves be its author and finisher."

Then the guards had prodded Chamberlain in one direction while Lincoln was led off in another.

It was 1863. The fate of the Republic had taken an ugly turn just over two score years ago when its military had fully become an arm of politics. Now, Chamberlain reflected bitterly, his own fate had been changed for the next forty years by the curiosity which had led him to seek the truth about the early years of his nation, and by his inability to keep his mouth shut in the face of injustice.

Except for an occasional thump with a rifle butt or sharp prod with the point of bayonet, Chamberlain's guards paid him little attention as he was ushered into a holding pen crowded with those in a mix of garb. "They'll not dress us as convicts?" someone asked in a broad Midwestern accent.

"No," another person carrying Boston in his every word replied. "Uniforms cost money. We'll wear what we were arrested in, and die in rags."

"No talking!" a pompous man in a Navy officer's uniform announced. The uniform was immaculate, unmarred by any actual service at sea, and bore a political party badge on the left breast.

"The military took an oath to the Constitution once," Chamberlain said. "Not to their parties or to their leaders. To the Constitution."

"Silence!" the officer bellowed, his words this time reinforced by a group of soldiers who waded into the holding cell, yanking out prisoners.

Chamberlain found himself led to a platform where a prison train awaited. He was shoved inside one of the cars, pushed into an aisle seat, and menaced with a bayonet poised near his nose as his right leg was shackled to the left leg of a man already seated next to the window.

His new companion wore a military uniform like those of the guards, but one from which all insignia, badges and rank had been stripped. He was older than Chamberlain, with a courtly air despite the indignity of his current position.

Despite an urge to speak to his companion in misery, Chamberlain managed to keep quiet this time as the guards roamed the aisle of the car. More prisoners were brought in and chained to their seatmates until the car was full.

When he had been brought to this confinement facility Chamberlain had himself been hooded, unable to tell what time of day it was. Now he saw the sun halfway down the sky. He had eaten nothing for at least a day and a half, but there were no signs of provisions aboard this train.

At least he could appreciate the irony of an until-recently professor from Bowdoin College looking forward to arrival at a plantation, doomed to hard labor in the fields, in the hopes that he would finally be fed something.

Once everyone had been chained and the car was full, the haste of the loading and shackling was replaced by inactivity. Guards and prisoners sat waiting as the afternoon wore away and it grew hotter inside the train. No one told them anything and nothing appeared to be going on.

The sun had sunk toward the horizon when the shouts of orders sounded, rousing Chamberlain from a drowse born of heat, lack of food and exhaustion. The train jerked into motion, rumbling out of the facility and heading south.

As the prison train rolled across the Potomac river in the last rays of the setting sun, Chamberlain gazed through the bars of the window next to his companion. The view was a restricted one, but he could see lights springing to life on one of the forts surrounding

Washington, DC. The lights, and the cannon they served, pointed both outward and inward, protecting and menacing the capital in equal measure. The image epitomized the United States, Chamberlain thought, a supposedly free land held in thrall by those who were charged to protect it, those jailors themselves answering to a few powerful men rather than to the will of the people.

*What if Jefferson had chosen to handle things differently? If he had controlled Burr, and responded to Adams' partisan packing of the military officer corps in some non-partisan manner? Would the country be different today, more like that which Washington had championed by example?*

*Would people like Lincoln, and me, be prisoners? Would our generals still all come from the ranks of the wealthy and our wealthy all come from the ranks of our generals? Would slavery still dominate the economies of not only the south but of all other portions of the country?*

*Useless, idle conjecture. It did not happen, and here I sit in chains.*

As the noise of the train became loud enough to cover conversation, the older man seated next to Chamberlain finally spoke. His stripped uniform no longer offered clues to his origin, but his accent identified the man as being from one of the southern states. "Enjoy the sights, sir. There is little to be seen of the world when stooping over the crops in a plantation's fields."

"I never thought I would be regretting not being sentenced to imprisonment in Fortress Monroe," Chamberlain admitted.

"While confinement and labor at Fortress Monroe may not be as openly brutal as a plantation, you would not be enjoying picnics there, sir, and though the fort is almost surrounded by water, none of that can be seen from the cells."

Chamberlain managed a small, brief smile. "Irony is our constant companion in the so-called land of liberty, sir. What brings a military officer to this state, for so I judge you to be? What was your offense?"

"A former officer," the other corrected, his mouth twisting at the words. "I refused an unlawful order, one which would have required me to violate the Constitution. After a brief show-trial for treason in front of the hooded judges of one of the military tribunals, here I sit beside you, bound for servitude for the crimes of believing in liberty and in the Republic."

They had both kept their voices low so they wouldn't be heard far over the rumble of the train, but one of the soldiers standing guard at the end of their car gave Chamberlain a hard look. Chamberlain pretended to stare out the barred window again for a while. As the train proceeded south and west into Virginia the buildings of Washington had given way to thickly forested land on either side of the rail line, the dark masses of trees only occasionally yielding begrudgingly to a clearing holding a building or a small town whose lights revealed little.

Finally, as the guard's attention wandered, Chamberlain's new companion spoke again. "And your offense, sir?"

"I conducted research," Chamberlain admitted. "I gained access to the papers of George Washington, and to histories from the period immediately after our country was founded, and learned that General Washington was not installed as President by the army as our schools are required to teach, but instead rejected such an authority and only became president as a result of open, fair and free elections."

"Treasonous sentiments, indeed," his companion murmured. "Were you foolish enough to tell others?"

"I was. And one of them, it seems, reported that I was a danger." The former officer eyed Chamberlain. "Are you a danger?"

"Only to oppression. Only to lies. Those who rule our country are betraying everything for which our forefathers fought," Chamberlain declared in a whisper. "Others in the north talk of revolt, but I hoped to change the country by words, by argument and the appeal to truth. Perhaps fighting is all we have left, though there's little chance of that once we are chain-ganged into servitude."

"Perhaps. But do not forget that the negroes have risen more than once. You have not heard? A free press would have reported it and accurate histories recorded it, but not when the government claims secrecy for anything that might embarrass it. No, sir, the slaves of this country have not accepted their fate meekly, and if they can still resist, so can we." His companion looked up as two of the soldier guards marched down the center aisle of the rail car.

One of the guards leveled the bayonet on the end of his rifle until it aimed between Chamberlain's eyes. "Orders are to remain quiet!"

Speaking had only brought him trouble. Wisdom once more dictated silence. *But a man can only stay silent for so long.* Chamberlain glared at the guard. "Whose orders? By what right does any man order silence when the Constitution of the United States of America grants the right of free speech to all?"

The guard looked startled by both the defiance and the question, but then an overweight officer in a new and ill-fitting uniform pushed up beside him and gave Chamberlain a contemptuous look. "We are defending this country against those who would threaten it, and that includes such as you who have been tried and found guilty. Remain silent or—"

"Tried?" Chamberlain cried. He knew from the man's appearance that the officer was another political hack recently appointed to the military based on his loyalty to party rather than to country or constitution. "Before a panel of hooded officers, with no lawyer permitted me, with no chance to view the evidence made against me, and no right to speak on my own behalf? Those who founded this country would be sickened by those who claim to act for the Republic but are worse in their actions than any agent of King George III ever aspired to be!"

The officer's face reddened. "I am a major in the Army of the United States and I will not tolerate such disrespect!"

Chamberlain's companion laughed softly. "Major?" he drawled. "From the looks of you, two days ago you were rounding up mandatory contributions for politicians. You're no soldier. You wouldn't have lasted one minute at West Point. But I would have dearly enjoyed dealing with you there."

This time the major's face grew so dark it seemed to purple, but before he could speak the brakes squealed and everyone was thrown forward as the train lurched to a screaming halt. The major and the guards were still disentangling themselves when the door at the front of the car banged open and another soldier looked in. "Tree across the track! A big one! The colonel says to send two men from each car to help clear it!"

Grumbling, the major told off two of the guards and sent them out, then stomped grandly to the front of the car and vented his wrath on the remaining guards until the door to the car swung open again.

The major turned his head to snarl at the latest arrival, but instead paled as a pistol barrel touched his nose.

Several men followed the pistol barrel into the car, shotguns and pistols coming to bear on the rest of the guards while the soldiers were still trying to swing around the long barrels of their rifles. Within moments the guards had been disarmed and were being bound.

One of the intruders was a tall, handsome man who carried himself in a way that made Chamberlain think of some Knight of the Round Table. He walked down the aisle of the car, indicating prisoners who his followers hastened to release with keys taken from the major. Reaching Chamberlain's row, the man looked down at the southerner chained to him and laughed. "Hullo, Lo."

"Good evening, Win," Chamberlain's companion replied cheerfully. "It has been a while. What brings you here?"

"The colonel. He heard you would be on this train."

Another man rushed into the car and saluted the handsome gentleman. "The train is ours, major."

"Damn fine work, sergeant. Our work here will be done soon. Are you ready to go, Lo?"

Chamberlain's companion stood up, then gestured to Chamberlain. "Please bring my new friend as well."

"Oh?" The major eyed Chamberlain. "Who is he?"

Chamberlain answered. "Professor of Rhetoric Joshua Chamberlain. From Bowdoin, in Maine."

"The hell you say." The tall, handsome major flashed a grin at the southerner. "Come along, then, professor. I do not know what services a professor of rhetoric can render our cause, but if Lo vouches for you that is all I require."

Chamberlain joined the stream of released prisoners as they left the train and followed guides into the woods. After several minutes, he looked back through the trees and saw the lights of the train moving off. "They're just letting the train depart?" he asked.

"As far as the trestle across the James River," the good-looking officer replied. "Have introductions been made? What is this country coming to? I am Major Winfield Hancock of the Army of the New Republic, professor, and this is Captain Lewis Armistead, still of the regular army as far as I know, if you haven't been formally introduced to him, either. Our men will take the train as far as the trestle, then set fire to it and burn both bridge and train."

Chamberlain felt a chill which had nothing to do with the night air. "What of the people on the train?"

Hancock waved one hand dismissively. "We've already let the other prisoners from the train go to scatter into the woods where they may. The soldiers will be released before the train is set afire." His smile shone white in the darkness. "There's little sense in killing the so-called officers on that train. Such buffoons are more a danger to the side they serve than to us."

"Where are we going, Win?" Armistead asked.

"To the colonel's headquarters for the night. There are horses up ahead. Don't worry, even in the dark his men know this region like the backs of their hands."

"The colonel?" Armistead pressed.

"Mosby," Hancock replied. "John Singleton Mosby. A damned fine tactician and strategist. He rules this part of Virginia, and he's no friend of tyranny."

"I have heard the name, but not that he was a colonel."

"That's his current rank in the Army of the New Republic. We're growing, Lo. More volunteers every day. Even here in northern Virginia some folks are getting fed up with the regular army deciding who the president will be and the president doing whatever he thinks the army wants and never mind the Constitution."

"There are some in Maine as well," Chamberlain offered. "We are a long ways from Washington and that has made it less galling, but the free folk of Maine are getting less and less tolerant of a federal government dancing to the tune set by plantation lords in the south and rich industrialists in the north." He suddenly remembered where Armistead was from. "My apologies if my statement offended you, Captain Armistead."

Armistead waved away Chamberlain's apology. "You say nothing but the truth, professor. There is no need for concern on my account when speaking candidly."

"Don't let Lo's mild manners fool you," Hancock cautioned. "This old bastard has a temper. Just ask Jubal Early."

"Speaking of fatherless get," Armistead murmured. "I only regret that the plate I broke over his head was not made of pewter rather than porcelain." He smiled briefly at Chamberlain. "That small event led to my departure from West Point. I received a commission later on despite that, but unlike my esteemed friend Winfield Hancock I never graduated from the Point."

"It doesn't make you any less an officer," Hancock declared. "Especially compared to a son-of-a-bitch like Early. Remember when his men tried to blow him to hell during the war with Mexico? Rolled a cannon ball with a lit fuse under his cot. Damned if I know how he survived."

"The devil looks after his own."

They reached a clearing where Chamberlain could make out many horses through the dimness. He was led to one and mounted it, then watched as a large group of already-mounted men rode into the clearing. "Report, Captain Buford," Hancock called.

"Our maneuvers were successful, Major," Buford announced. "Regular army cavalry patrols were drawn off and are currently chasing their own tails well to the northeast of here. I have a screen of scouts in place to let us know if any veer back in this direction."

"Damn good job, John. Have your men take the lead. I'll follow with the raiding force."

Armistead, his horse near Chamberlain's, turned a surprised expression on Hancock. "I thought John Buford was still out west."

"Was," Hancock agreed. "Fighting the damned Texicans. He was relieved of command after refusing to follow a lunatic order from a politician in a colonel's uniform. Then he had to watch his company of cavalry get torn to pieces in a senseless charge, and endure being court-martialed for the crime of trying to prevent that. They tried busting him to sergeant, but Buford rode away with most of what was left of his company."

"You cannot underestimate the Texicans," Armistead said, sighing. "They show no enthusiasm for accepting the annexation of their republic by our republic, and all too much enthusiasm for fighting anyone who disagrees with them."

"You all seem to know each other," Chamberlain marveled.

Armistead and Hancock exchanged looks. "West Point, professor," Armistead explained. "Despite the common use by the government in Washington of military officer positions as reward for political loyalty, the regular army has managed to maintain a few officers on merit, almost all West Point graduates."

"It sounds like many of you are going over to the Army of the New Republic."

"More and more," Hancock said quietly. "All of us? Not so. And not every professional sticking with the government is a son-of-a-bitch like Early or a dumb-ass incompetent like Pope. There's some very good men who still march to the beat of the drum in Washington. Make no mistake of that." He paused, then spoke with sudden passion. "May God damn Andrew Jackson! If not for him, we would still be a republic in fact as well as name, and not facing our own former comrades at point of sword."

"Most blame Jackson," Chamberlain objected, "but even though the use of military officer positions as partisan political prizes bore its awful fruit after Andrew Jackson, the tree was planted by John Adams. Adams was one of the founders we revere, yet he was too free with the idea of emergency measures which overrode the Constitution, such as the Alien and Sedition Acts. Now we live in a perpetual state of national emergency, subject to 'protections' which have produced the loss of the liberty which we mourn."

Armistead nodded. "Even though West Pointers have protected each other somewhat, it has been a losing battle, more of us being forced out each year. We still have a core of actual professional officers trying to hold things together, but the rest of the officer corps is simply a group of political partisans who come and go at the whims of those pulling the strings at the White House."

"Thank you, professor." Hancock looked straight ahead as he spoke. "I had not heard some of what you say, which is little surprise given how much of our history has been hidden for the benefit of those controlling public records. But the blame scarcely matters now except to prevent a repeat of the tragedy. What counts for us is the cure, and that is something in which we must all have a hand if the republic is to be renewed."

"Someone else said much the same to me recently," Chamberlain said, recalling Lincoln's words.

They rode in silence for a long time, Chamberlain catching glimpses of the stars overhead through the thick tree cover and thinking on what Hancock had said. Had he included Chamberlain when Hancock spoke of all of them having to work for the new republic? It seemed wrong to expect men such as this to sacrifice while Chamberlain sought safe passage back to Maine to hide among those who knew him. But Chamberlain's mind kept shying away from the answer. He was not a military man. He had studied history and read some manuals, but that was the extent of his knowledge of war.

The night and the forest seemed interminable, stretching forever, Chamberlain's belly painfully reminding him of how long it had been since he last ate. But none of those around him complained, and Chamberlain felt a reluctance to appear weaker than them.

Finally the large group of mounted men rode out onto a wider road, then not long afterwards into a town in which a few windows still showed lights despite the late hour.

The group broke up, men dismounting and heading in all directions with the horses, Chamberlain staying with Armistead and Hancock as the two headed for a large house. Inside, food awaited the men, along with another officer whom Hancock saluted. "Objective accomplished, colonel. No casualties."

"Good. The raid I led against a federal depot near Manassas was also successful as more than another diversion. We acquired a number of new rifles and a good supply of shot and powder. Captain Armistead, I am gratified that we were able to prevent you from being subjected to a miscarriage of justice."

Armistead saluted as well. "Unfortunately, the miscarriage goes deeper than imprisonment. I was also stripped of rank and expelled from the service."

Hancock chuckled. "Damn it all, Lo, the Army of the New Republic can always use another captain, especially one as good as you."

"I concur," the colonel agreed. He turned toward Chamberlain. "And you are, sir?"

"Professor Joshua Chamberlain." Chamberlain shook hands with the colonel, feeling awkward, and trying desperately not to lunge toward the food resting on a nearby table. "You are a professional soldier, too, sir?"

Mosby looked offended. "Not I. You see before you a former felon and a former lawyer."

"And yet a damned decent human being nonetheless," Hancock observed. "As well as the most brilliant master of unorthodox tactics I have ever encountered."

"How did you end up here?" Chamberlain asked as Mosby waved him to a seat at the table. With more control than he thought he could muster, Chamberlain began to eat and drink slowly.

"I might ask the same of you, sir." Mosby shrugged, then smiled. "There is plenty to eat here. Do not stint yourself. I know the government does not care to waste money on feeding prisoners bound for the plantations. As you have also doubtless discovered, professor, an independent mind is not a virtue in the eyes of our current government. As one who served time in prison, and narrowly escaped time on a plantation myself, over a little matter of shooting a fellow student when I was much younger and more impulsive, I am keen on questions of justice. As a lawyer, this led me to attempt to defend those the government did not wish defended. A timely warning allowed me to escape my own arrest, and since then I have found other ways to fight tyranny." Mosby patted the pistol by his side.

"Yet we still do too little," Hancock grumbled through a mouthful of chicken.

"We cannot raise the Army of the New Republic overnight," Mosby replied. "It takes time and training, and the need to do all in secrecy while the government hunts us further complicates the task."

"Secrecy, indeed," Armistead commented. "I have heard little but rumors of your actions in this part of Virginia."

"Control of the press makes it an ally of the government in hiding inconvenient facts," Mosby remarked. "We have caused our rulers trouble enough already, and we are not alone, Captain Armistead. The Army of the New Republic grows in silence, mostly in states to the north but elsewhere as well. The Texican Republic has not been subdued. Every time the US Army defeats one of their armies, Sam Houston raises a new army. California remains in contention despite officially being part of the country. The Californians keep fighting, and they divert enough gold from official accounts to allow them to buy weapons and support from overseas."

Hancock nodded. "The army of the west isn't making much progress in California what with the freedom fighters in Kansas Territory harassing their supply lines, and the Mormon militias doing the same through Deseret." He grinned. "Nor can having that damned fool McClellan in command help them."

"Especially with Early commanding in Texas," Mosby agreed. "Both of them have their own eyes on the White House, neither wants the other to gain it, and so they work against each other. Our enemies can be the best friends of liberty."

Armistead now looked from Hancock to Mosby. "I would join your army, if you will have me. The cause is just, and I hated not being in the same army as you, Win."

Hancock smiled again. "I felt the same, Lo."

"We will do a formal swearing-in tomorrow," Mosby said. "We also have some new enlisted recruits. We're staying in this town another day to rest, then we will move on before the federals hear of our location."

The next day Chamberlain watched Armistead and a collection of men of varied ages take the oath to join the Army of the New Republic. Soon afterwards, Captain Buford led out a mounted patrol to scout for activity by the federals. Chamberlain feared feeling isolated among these soldiers, but they made him welcome, asking about sentiment in Maine regarding the federal government. Though Chamberlain assured them that Maine was no less discontented than any other state, he felt a growing sense of personal dissatisfaction, a feeling that he should be doing something to match the dedication of these men to liberty.

That evening Chamberlain was pleased to be invited to dine with Mosby, Hancock and Armistead again. He spoke little, listening instead as the three officers spoke casually of past battles and experiences. Chamberlain felt as if he were in a play or a dream, or somehow cast into the past, seated among English barons from the days of King John, or Roundheads in the time of Charles I, or even beside Lafayette as the French cavalier sat with Washington himself. Surely those combatants of old had spoken like this, shared the same humor and the same tales of misfortune or success, as they had discussed the overthrow of the corrupt monarchs of their time. No, it felt more like being among the Patriots themselves, those who had plotted revolution in taverns in Boston. *We mutually pledge to each other our Lives, our Fortunes, and our sacred Honor.*

"You seem pensive this evening, sir," Mosby observed.

Jarred from his reverie, Chamberlain nodded, smiling slightly. "I was thinking, sir, of the last time a man named Hancock plotted rebellion against unjust and unelected authority."

Major Hancock leaned back in his seat, grinning. "I never could sign my name as well as that other Hancock, but I don't think he could sit a horse half so well as me, so I've no grounds for complaint."

"John Hancock was also wealthy," Armistead pointed out.

"I am wealthy in friends," Hancock declared, "and if any of you sons of bitches dare to disagree that you are my friend then I will see you on the field on honor and blow your damned fool head off."

They were still laughing when a quick knock announced the arrival of a volunteer soldier, who whispered a message to Colonel Mosby. "We have a visitor," Mosby announced to the others. "Bring him in," he ordered. The soldier went to the door and beckoned to someone outside, then held the door before leaving as a dour-looking man entered and nodded gruffly to everyone.

"James?" Hancock asked in surprise. "I'll be damned."

"Doubtless," the visitor answered. "Long time, Win."

"Yes, it has been a long time." Hancock glanced at Mosby and Chamberlain. "This is Captain James Longstreet, West Point class of '42. I haven't heard much of you recently, James."

"I left the army over a year ago." Longstreet sat where Mosby indicated and stretched out his legs with a sigh, gratefully accepting the offer of food and drink. "It was either that or shoot my commanding officer."

"Early?" Armistead asked.

"Nah. I would have shot Early, and then left. I was under McClellan. Useless is too kind a word. He's got his eyes on the

White House, and is so scared of not getting it that he won't fight a battle he might lose. Which is every battle." Longstreet grinned derisively. "I didn't know you were with this bunch, Lo."

"I just came in from a prison train, headed for the plantations."

Longstreet stared glumly at Armistead for a moment before shaking his head. "There you have it. When an officer like you can be sent to the plantations, what have we come to? I couldn't support it any longer."

"I heard you had gone back to Alabama," Hancock offered.

"Yeah, tried that. It wasn't really home though. Besides, you know me, Win. Wherever I am, folks start wishing I was somewhere else. My opinions are too well known because I can't keep my mouth shut. The federals came looking for me and the local authorities in the south all thought locking me up sounded like a good idea since they and the federals march to the same tune. I headed north through Tennessee and Kentucky until I found a bunch of like-minded folks in Illinois, where the federal government isn't so well regarded. Do you remember Grant, Win?"

"Grant? Ulysses? He left the service about ten years ago, didn't he?"

"Yeah." Longstreet sat silent for a moment, his eyes on the flame of the lamp. "I always thought Grant steady but unremarkable. He's got an army now, though. You know he's been raising volunteers for the Army of the New Republic, but I doubt you've heard how many. When Grant sends the word out, he'll have five thousand men under arms, enough to overwhelm every regular army garrison in Illinois."

"Five thousand?" Mosby trained an admiring look on Longstreet. "You're working with him?"

"Second in command. Cump Sherman…you remember him, Win…has a few thousand volunteers in Indiana ready to rise as well. He's coordinating closely with Grant and me. That's another reason I'm down here. The Army of the New Republic has been a lot of groups, most of them small, operating independently. We're going to have to work together, establish a true command structure. Grant, Sherman and I are trying to lay the groundwork for that."

"Cump's joined the Army of the New Republic?" Hancock asked. "That shouldn't surprise me. The cocky bastard never did care for rules."

"If anyone wishes to exercise authority over my actions, they must first prove their legitimacy and competence to me," Mosby cautioned.

A rare smile lighted Longstreet's face for a moment. "Grant told me to ask you to just keep on doing what you've been doing."

Mosby smiled back. "That request I can agree to without hesitation. When will you rise?"

"That's the problem." Longstreet shook his head, morose once more. "We can raise a small army. What we can't do is tell the people of the state why they should support us rather than the current federal government. To them, we're all too likely to look like just another batch of soldiers planning on running the government. We need someone who can talk well, a civilian who's known to be honest and can make the right speeches and the right arguments to win popular sentiment, to convince the people we really mean it when we talk about restoring the republic and getting the army out of politics."

"We have a professor of rhetoric here," Hancock said, with a half-bow toward Chamberlain. "He can doubtless offer up many fine words which would put us crude soldiers to shame."

Longstreet frowned as if he didn't get the humor. "We know who we need. Someone who we know the people of Illinois and surrounding states will believe. Grant sent me here to see if you had him, though I had hell's own time finding you."

"Had him?" Mosby asked. "Why would we have this individual?"

"We know you've been raiding the prison trains bound south. This man was arrested and brought to DC. We know that much, and assumed he was sent south after that. Fellow name of Lincoln."

"Lincoln?" Chamberlain asked in surprise. "Abraham Lincoln?"

"Yes." Longstreet squinted at Chamberlain. "Who are you again, sir?"

"Professor Chamberlain. From Bowdoin. In Maine."

"Oh. Yes. Abraham Lincoln. Known and trusted in Illinois. Most important, a fine speaker and a true believer in the republic. We know that. We need to get him back to Illinois to rally the people to us, and we need him as soon as may be. The volunteers are growing restless. Jobs are being sent to factories near planta- tions in the south and out west where slaves can do the work for less than even the pitiful wages paid up north by those who say they must compete with slave-labor. Families are suffering, folks losing homes and farms while the bankers make more money every day off their misery, and it's getting hard to hold our volunteers back. It would be a disaster if the volunteers act before we have the means to convince the rest of the people of our motives."

"I remember the name of Lincoln now," Mosby said. "We've seen some pamphlets with Lincoln's speeches on them that got smuggled down this way. The man does have a fine way with words." Mosby shook his head. "But we do not intercept every train. We must have missed the one Lincoln was on."

"He did not go by train," Chamberlain said, drawing surprised glances again. "He was sent to Fortress Monroe as a prisoner."

Everyone looked at Chamberlain in silence for a moment, then Mosby spoke with a hint of skepticism. "How do you know this, sir?"

"We went before the same tribunal. I was in the room when he was sentenced. Rendition to Fortress Monroe." Chamberlain felt awkward at the way these men were hanging on his words, yet also pleased that he was contributing in some small way to their efforts. "We spoke very briefly before being separated."

"Hmmm," Longstreet observed. "Good-lookin' fella, would you say?"

"Lincoln?" Chamberlain asked. "No. No, that is one thing I cannot say. His words are far handsomer than he is."

Longstreet nodded. "You did meet the man in truth, then."

Hancock spoke up. "Fortress Monroe? Do you know how they were sending him there?"

Chamberlain tried to recall the words spoken by the judges at the tribunal. "They mentioned the *Merrimac*. They said it was leaving for Hampton Roads the day after the train I was on left Washington, and Lincoln should be put on it."

"A warship," Mosby said. "One of the steam frigates. If Lincoln is as important a prisoner as we have been told, they would have sent him by such means rather than risking overland travel. If the *Merrimac* left Baltimore today she would probably have arrived at Fortress Monroe before nightfall."

"He's there now, then," Longstreet said. "We feared that he had been hanged or shot already."

"They said," Chamberlain replied, "the judges at the tribunal that is, that they did not want Lincoln to be a martyr. They wanted to keep him in prison indefinitely."

Longstreet stared at the lamp again. "They might succeed in that. Fortress Monroe. Helluva strong place."

"Damned helluva strong place," Hancock agreed.

"You need Lincoln?" Mosby asked.

"We do," Longstreet said. "He's not a handsome man, but he's an honest one. No offense, Win, but it is far easier to find handsome men than honest ones. Lincoln can unite the people behind us. The people up north anyway. I don't know about the south."

"Yes, you do," Armistead commented. "The ones running the federal government have long made cause with the slave-holding aristocracy in the south. Neither of them want anything to change, neither want a free country with open democracy, and a permanent state of military emergency suits the slave-holders just fine. They will try to convince the people of the south to back the federal government, and many will believe them and fight for them for fear of revolution and lawlessness."

"If I had that many slaves in my backyard, I would fear lawlessness more than tyranny, too," Hancock said. "Lo, we're also talking about Virginia here."

"I know it, Win." Armistead glared at the floor. "But it would not be Virginia I would be fighting. It would be the federal government run by the mighty and the wealthy, and the ones in Virginia willing to continue running that government as a tyranny that keeps Virginia and all other states in bondage. To free Virginia, I must fight."

Mosby nodded. "There is truth in that, sir. Who here knows much about Fortress Monroe?"

Hancock and Armistead both stood, then each deferred mockingly to the other before they jointly bent over the table and sketched out a diagram. Chamberlain craned to look, seeing a rough hexagon with six irregularly spaced arrow-shaped fortifications projecting from its sides. "As James said," Armistead explained, "Fort Monroe is a mighty fortification of modern design. The walls are high and thick, this moat around the walls is deep and wide, and there are only three narrow causeways into the fort, at roughly these locations. It would require an army to besiege and take that fortress, and the Navy warships in Hampton Roads would use their artillery to support the fort as well."

"Who's in command there now?" Mosby asked.

"Colonel Lee, who also helped design the final fortifications a decade ago."

Longstreet grimaced. "Bobbie Lee is no fool. He's a skilled professional, doubtless assigned to command the fortress because all of the political factions in Washington know he favors none and can be trusted to keep imprisoned all sent to him."

"How many men does he have?"

Armistead answered again. "A regiment, supposedly, but it was always understrength, carrying only five companies on its rolls. About six months ago the regiment was ordered to send two of those companies to the Army of the West. Replacements were promised, but all here know how rarely those actually appear with the army fighting on two fronts as well as dealing with all of the volunteers such as us. If I were a betting man, I would wager that Lee still only has three companies remaining to man the fort."

"That is thin, but it's plenty enough to keep us out." Mosby frowned in thought. "Everyone knows that Fortress Monroe is invincible. That's a weakness. Overconfidence and surety are deadly conceits." Mosby looked around. "But how would we overcome the fort's defenses?"

"With what we have? It could not be done, not in a fair fight," Armistead declared.

Mosby smiled. "I fight to win, sir."

"Good enough, but the walls and the moat remain."

An idea popped into Chamberlain's head as he thought of getting through walls which could not be breached. "A Trojan horse?"

Everyone looked at him, then Mosby nodded. "A subterfuge can get us through walls which are proof against any artillery we could bring to bear. But what subterfuge? What could get into that fort?"

After a moment's thought, Hancock grinned. "A regular cavalry force, sent south to hunt that traitor Mosby and his evil compatriots. Arriving in the dead of night with forged orders. We've got enough uniforms for men and regulation tack for horses to put together almost a full company that will look official in the dark. Once we were inside, with most of the garrison asleep, we could gain control of the fort long enough to free the prisoners, including Lincoln."

There was silence as everyone considered the idea, then Longstreet shook his head gloomily. "Even if you arrive in the middle of the night, Bobbie Lee will have left standing orders to awaken him in such an event. He'll come to see you and your orders, and he knows everyone here. Once he recognizes one of us, the game will be over, and no enlisted trooper can play an officer convincingly enough to fool Bobbie Lee."

"He doesn't know me," Mosby replied. "That gives us one officer."

"Two," Chamberlain heard himself saying. "He doesn't know me, either."

Once again he became the center of attention, then Armistead smiled. "You would be willing to participate in this operation, Professor Chamberlain?"

"Yes." Chamberlain swallowed nervously, then nodded. "It's important. I will do what I can."

Hancock frowned appraisingly at Chamberlain. "You've got the right bearing and style of speaking to play an officer. Can you, though?"

"I've taken on roles, sir, in speeches. This would be another role."

"A role which might cost you your life, sir, and one upon which the lives of many others will depend."

"I will do what I can as best I can," Chamberlain repeated. "I can do no less than the rest of you."

Mosby nodded. "Your spirit is right for the role. Our West Pointers will teach you the exact ways to act and the language you must use. We will attempt this, gentlemen. I tire of fighting on the margins, pricking the hide of the enemy but causing no real damage. The cause of freedom requires that we run greater risks and strike greater blows." He stood up, pointing to the diagram of Fort Monroe. "Captain Longstreet says we must get Lincoln back to Illinois as soon as we can. Tomorrow we will start assembling our force of counterfeit government cavalry and moving toward Norfolk. With luck, we will strike Fortress Monroe within a week's time."

He raised his glass. "To victory, gentlemen."

The others raised their glasses as well, Longstreet adding a gruff addendum. "Or death."

Hancock smiled again before downing his drink. "Or both victory and death, damn it! Welcome to the cause, professor."

**SIX DAYS LATER,** Chamberlain rode a horse through the night's darkness toward one of the causeways leading into Fort Monroe. He wore the uniform of a captain in the regular army cavalry, a pistol holstered on one hip and a regulation saber in a scabbard on the other. The unfamiliar weight of the weapons made him less uncomfortable than the fact that he was riding at the head of the column pretending to be a company of regular cavalry. Mosby had decided that, given the chance Lee might recognize him from drawings on wanted posters, it would be better for someone totally unknown to Lee to pose as the commanding officer of the cavalry. Mosby was riding several files behind him now, close enough to intervene if things started to fall apart, but Chamberlain still felt alone as the northernmost gate to the fort loomed ever closer.

They had already made it through two checkpoints tonight on the road to the fort, the sentries at both places waving through the column without a hint of suspicion. But the fort itself would be a more challenging encounter, so Chamberlain did his best to fall into the role of an officer who had recently been awarded his rank for political achievements. Any errors he made should be attributed to his inexperience by the regular soldiers in the fort.

Two sentries stood forth as the mounted column neared the gate, one of them calling out a challenge. Chamberlain raised one hand as he had been taught by Buford. "Column halt!" As he reined in his own mount and the rest of the cavalry clattered to a stop behind him, Chamberlain answered the challenge, his voice clear and confident in the quiet of the night. "Third Company, Tenth Cavalry, Captain Green commanding, here on orders from the War Department."

The sergeant in charge of the sentries came close to look at Chamberlain in the light of a lantern the sergeant held high. After a brief examination, the sergeant saluted. "Good evening, sir. I'll have to call the officer in charge of the watch. We didn't receive any word that you were coming."

"That's because it was a secret movement, sergeant," Chamberlain declared with self-important superiority. "Fetch your officer."

Waiting was doubly hard because he had to appear self-assured despite his fears. But it was only a few minutes before a lieutenant came hastening out of the gate and saluted Chamberlain. "Lieutenant Walker, Captain of the Guard, sir. May I see your orders, sir?"

Chamberlain returned the salute with the hint of casualness that Hancock had drilled him on, offering the orders which Mosby's forgers had crafted. "It's late, lieutenant," he prodded.

"Yes, sir. I'm certain the captain will understand that I have to proceed according to the fort commander's standing orders, sir." The lieutenant read the orders carefully, then examined the column behind Chamberlain as best he could in the dark. "Are there civilians back there, sir?"

"A few prisoners," Chamberlain explained as if bored.

"Welcome to Fort Monroe, sir. Your men may enter, though I request they dismount and lead their horses. I will notify Colonel Lee of your arrival."

Longstreet had been right about that. "There's no need to disturb the colonel's sleep on our account," Chamberlain suggested.

"Thank you, sir, but I am required to notify him. Please rest your command in the courtyard inside the gate while I inform Colonel Lee and he provides direction for your billeting and the disposal of your prisoners."

As the lieutenant strode quickly away, Chamberlain turned to face his column. "Dismount! Follow in a column of threes!" If he hadn't been so nervous, this military officer's role would have been a pleasurable thing.

Chamberlain led the way into the fort, noticing as they passed through the gate just how thick were the walls to either side of it. As Armistead had said, this was a fortress which could have held out as long as Troy. But like Troy, its guardians were allowing a disguised enemy to breach those walls.

"My men need to water their mounts," Chamberlain insisted to the guard sergeant once all of the supposed cavalry force was inside the fort. Mosby had assumed they might need an excuse to get some of the false cavalrymen out of sight of the gate sentries.

The sergeant looked around, but there was no officer here to back him up, and Chamberlain's request was perfectly reasonable. He nodded. "You can send them a few at a time to the troughs, sir."

Chamberlain faced his column, his eyes searching for Mosby. "Lieutenant, we're to wait for Colonel Lee. Send the men in small groups to water their mounts."

They waited under the starlight, the men silent but the horses stamping and blowing occasionally. Mosby told off detachments to go water their horses, and none of the sentries noticed that in each group fewer men came back each time than had gone out. Chamberlain had to fight down a powerful urge to scan the darkness for those men, whom he knew would be moving stealthily to surprise the sentries on the walls and ensure there were no sentries at the other two gates which should be sealed for the night.

Finally, Chamberlain saw the lieutenant returning with another officer. In the light of the lieutenant's lantern, Chamberlain could see that Colonel Robert E. Lee was an older and courtly man, reminiscent of Captain Armistead but more elderly. His neatly trimmed hair and beard were a gray that stood out against Lee's dark blue uniform. Even if Chamberlain hadn't known that Lee was the product of generations of Southern aristocracy he would have guessed it from the man's appearance and attitude of unquestioned superiority. From all he had been told Lee had the brains and skills to justify that attitude, but it bothered Chamberlain to realize that Lee would have acted the same even if he had no claim but ancestry to authority. For the first time, Chamberlain realized that aristocracy wasn't simply a broad comparison, but a literally true description of how the upper class in the south saw themselves.

Distracted by these thoughts, Chamberlain barely remembered to salute first as Lee approached. Lee returned the salute slowly and precisely, turning to view the column of soldiers. "Tenth Cavalry? I was not told you were coming here, Captain Green."

"The War Department knows that Mosby's men intercept telegraphic messages, sir," Chamberlain explained. "We wished to surprise him and his bandits."

"It appears you did so," Lee agreed. He eyed Chamberlain. "I'm not familiar with your record, Captain Green."

Chamberlain puffed himself up in imitation of a self-important politician. "My commission is fairly recent, based upon my performance in the last presidential selection."

"I see." Lee's tone, only formal to this point, dropped several degrees toward freezing, but that was fine. The less he thought of Chamberlain's Captain Green persona the less he would hopefully concern himself with worries about this unheralded arrival of a cavalry company. "I will expect a full report in the morning, sir. You are to call on me promptly at nine o'clock."

"Yes, sir."

Lee turned to go, then paused, and instead pivoted toward the supposed prisoners. "How many men do you have, captain?"

"Eighty-one, sir."

"A bit understrength for such a mission. And how many prisoners?"

"An even dozen, sir."

"You took them without a fight?" Lee pressed. "In Mosby's territory?"

Chamberlain sank deeper into his role. "Of course there was a fight. I do not know what you are implying, sir."

"Surprise that your column was not cut to pieces, captain, with an inexperienced commanding officer and such small numbers moving through such a hazardous region, and that no word of your movements from any source came to us prior to this. You and your men are to wait here while I telegraph the War Department and find out more regarding this matter."

Mosby himself came up close to Lee. "I respectfully request that you remain here, colonel."

Lee frowned at Mosby, the sort of Olympian glower which must have reduced many a lower-ranking man to helplessness over the years. "Your request is insubordinate, lieutenant."

Mosby's pistol came up and centered between Lee's eyes. "I believe this outranks you, colonel. My request is now an order." To either side, the sentries and the lieutenant were also being menaced and their weapons taken by other false cavalrymen from the column. The supposed prisoners in the column also produced weapons of their own and moved to help guard the regulars. "All of the sentries on the walls have already been disarmed and taken prisoner while we waited. As long as everyone remains silent, no one shall be harmed, but if anyone makes a sound they will be the first to die."

Lee betrayed no fear, his icy gaze fixed on Mosby. "Do I know you, sir?"

Mosby inclined his head slightly toward Lee. "Colonel John Singleton Mosby of the Army of the New Republic, at your service, sir."

"You are no colonel. Neither are you a soldier. You are a bandit and a traitor to your country. When you are captured, you shall hang."

Mosby smiled, his teeth showing white in the darkness. "The capturing is the hard part, colonel."

"Colonel Lee." Chamberlain stepped forward, dropping his performance. "Surely you have seen that the government operates in violation of the Constitution of the Republic. You are being ordered to take actions contrary to the liberty our forefathers bequeathed us. If all good and honorable men would join in demanding that the government and the army abide by the Constitution and cease their tyrannical actions, then this country would be a republic of free men again in truth."

Lee turned his frosty gaze on Chamberlain. "And you are?"

"Joshua Chamberlain, Professor of Rhetoric, Bowdoin."

"Former professor, you mean to say," Lee corrected. "When you are taken prisoner, you will find a cell here awaits you."

"Better a cell here than the fields of a plantation! I was convicted of exercising free speech and other rights guaranteed by the Constitution! Nothing else! A professional such as yourself knows that partisan politics should have no role in the appointment and promotion of officers."

"You do not speak for me, sir. Freedom does not mean anarchy. I will stand by those who believe in the rule of law."

Chamberlain spread his hands. "You will not do the honorable thing, sir?"

Lee's face reddened. "I took an oath, sir. An oath to obey all lawful orders. Every action being ordered of me is in compliance with laws passed by the Congress, signed by the President and upheld by the Supreme Court. Can you say the same?"

"The congress is owned, the president installed by the army and the supreme court packed with those who would agree to any expansion of the power of the few at the expense of the many!"

"They are the laws of this land," Lee insisted.

Chamberlain shook his head. "This republic was founded by men who argued that unjust laws must be opposed."

"Do not lecture me on honor. A traitor, a civilian, a college professor, and a northerner. You have no concept of honor." Lee deliberately turned his back on Chamberlain.

Mosby, finishing giving orders for his men to release the prisoners in the fort, smiled at Chamberlain. "You could challenge him to a duel now."

"What would be the point of that?"

"If you were a southerner, you wouldn't even ask that question. But then if you were a southerner, you would know that men such as Lee who grow up owning slaves come to believe that all other men can be equally inferior to themselves. They also have very strong opinions on the protection of property, said property most importantly including slaves. He will not listen to any argument that you and I could make." Mosby gazed around ruefully. "As God is my witness, I would love to seize this fort and make a stand here. Imagine the ruckus that would raise. More than government censorship could cover up. But they would overwhelm us sooner or later, and we would have no means of retreat."

Chamberlain eyed the massive fortifications. "The defenders of the Alamo inspired the Texican Rebellion."

"Little good that did those defenders," Mosby noted dryly. "I am a fox, sir, and a fox does not allow himself to be trapped in a hole with no chance of escape."

"The fox has his wisdom," Chamberlain agreed. "I am in no position to argue with yours."

A man hurried up to Mosby. "There's no sign of anyone stirring in the barracks, colonel. We're watching the doors, but we can't seal them without making too much noise."

"Keep a close watch. How are the prisoners coming?"

Another man arrived just in time to answer that question. "Good, for the most part, but there's not nearly enough horses in the garrison for them all. We'll need to take some wagons."

"Hellfire and damnation," Mosby muttered. "Get the wagons ready. Quickly and quietly. Damn this night. It covers our movements but its silence betrays almost our every action. Chamberlain, go check on the released prisoners. Make certain that Lincoln is among them."

"Yes, colonel." Chamberlain ran toward where the cells should be, the sword scabbard slapping annoyingly against one leg until he reached down to hold on to it tightly. He found a crowd milling around, Mosby's men making constant efforts to keep everyone as silent as possible. Even in the darkness, one tall, thin shape stood out among the others. "Mr. Lincoln, sir?"

The man turned, revealing a familiar and homely face. "At your service, sir. You are not one of our jailors despite your garb. No! I see now that you are the one who spoke up at our mock trial. Life on the plantations did not suit you?"

Chamberlain could not help grinning at the question. "I was fortunate enough to escape the fate intended for me, Mr. Lincoln, and to find those who are friends to us and to the Republic. You are needed in Illinois, Mr. Lincoln."

"May I ask who it is who needs me?"

"The people of this country, sir."

A smile appeared and grew. While Lincoln was indeed unattractive, the smile transformed him as much as anything could. "I will serve no other masters, save liberty and the Republic governed by our Constitution. Can you get me to Illinois?"

"We will try, sir." A rattle of harness and creaking of wheels announced the arrival of four wagons with teams hitched to them, the sounds seeming to Chamberlain to echo in the night like the hammering of a blacksmith at work. Mosby's men boosted released prisoners into the wagons while Chamberlain stood back, watching but seeing no need to interfere. To his annoyance, though, Lincoln insisted on waiting until everyone else was in a wagon before taking a place in the last one.

When Chamberlain and the wagons reached the gate, Mosby's men were just finishing binding and gagging the regular soldiers who had been on sentry duty. Lee stood nearby.

Mosby spoke quietly to Lee. "Sir, will you give me your bond to remain silent on this spot until my men and I have departed this area?"

Lee did not look at Mosby as he answered. "I cannot in good conscience give my bond to a traitor and a bandit."

"Then I regret that my men will be required to bind and gag you, sir." Mosby motioned and his men began trussing Lee's hands.

Before they fastened a gag on Lee, the colonel turned to look at Chamberlain. "Mr. Chamberlain, I have been told that when you were taken from the prison train you were in company with an officer."

Chamberlain nodded. "Captain Armistead."

Lee hesitated. "I should be greatly in your debt if you would inform Captain Armistead that, should he surrender himself to me, I will ensure he is well treated and make every effort to see that his conviction is reversed."

"I will certainly pass on your words to Captain Armistead, sir," Chamberlain replied in a solemn voice. "However, I feel I must inform you that Captain Armistead appears unlikely to accept your offer. He has told me that he believes his honor requires his own present course of action."

Lee stood silent for a moment. "I deeply regret that. I hope Captain Armistead will reconsider. If I encounter him under other circumstances than his surrender, I will be forced to do my duty."

"I will tell him that as well, sir."

"Thank you, Mr. Chamberlain." Lee stoically endured having the gag placed on his mouth and having his legs bound, his eyes watching as Mosby's men mounted up, half of them preceding the wagons through the gate and the rest waiting for the wagons to pass through.

"Go with the lead element," Mosby ordered Chamberlain. "Play your role the rest of the night as well as you did until now and we shall see total success."

"Thank you, colonel." Chamberlain mounted, but as he started to ride through the gate heard a querulous voice sounding across the courtyard.

"Who ordered those wagons out?" Someone was standing in a doorway, his shape barely visible. "Captain of the guard! Where the hell are you?"

"Time to go," Mosby declared, waving Chamberlain and the rest of his men through the gate, then brought his horse around to answer the man. "Orders from Colonel Lee. We're sorry to have disturbed you, sir."

"Colonel Lee wouldn't have sent those wagons out without informing me! Why isn't the captain of the guard answering me? Where's Sergeant Pennington?"

"You'll have to ask them," Mosby answered. "Good evening, sir." With that, he spurred his horse through the gate and past the bound figures of the sentries and the captain of the guard. "On the double! The alarm will sound soon!"

The column had cleared the causeway and was clattering down the road away from the fort, the wagons making what seemed to be a cacophony of noise, when the report of a cannon boomed from one of the fort's walls, the echoes of its firing reverberating across the land and the waters of Hampton Roads. Chamberlain waited for the sound of shell but saw Mosby shaking his head. "That was an alarm, a gunshot meant to alert all defenders. The sleeping giant will awaken quickly now."

After half a minute the alarm was answered by a cannon fired on one of the warships anchored off shore, then several more cannon shots boomed near and far as the warning spread. The urgent summons of trumpets began sounding in what sounded like all directions as Mosby galloped to the front of the column and urged it to move faster, then headed back to ensure no one was falling behind.

The first check point loomed ahead, every soldier occupying it standing in or beside the road, rifles in hand. By a great effort, Chamberlain subdued the tremors in his voice so that it came out commanding as he yelled. "Raiders at the fort! Colonel Lee has sent us after them!"

The soldiers hesitated. "We haven't seen anyone!" one of them called back.

"We're moving to cut them off!" Chamberlain shouted. "Clear the road!"

With almost a hundred horsemen and four wagons bearing down on them, the half-dozen soldiers did as Chamberlain ordered, scrambling to the side of the road and watching the column tear past.

But at the second check point they encountered a barrier placed across the road, the soldiers manning the check point arrayed behind the barrier with rifles at ready. Chamberlain once again yelled at them to clear the road.

"Our orders are to halt all traffic!" the sergeant in charge of the check point replied. "Halt your column, sir!"

Chamberlain hesitated, but then Mosby was riding beside him, pistol in hand. "We have no time for bluffing, professor. There are probably a thousand men converging on this spot as we speak." Galloping up to the check point, he leveled his pistol at the sergeant. "Clear the road or we'll send you to hell!" Mosby cried.

The sergeant, with more courage than sense, tried to bring his rifle to bear. Mosby shot him, the other soldiers at the check point scattering as the horsemen stormed the barrier.

Unfortunately, it required a few moments for some of the riders to dismount, swing the barrier out of the way, and remount. The pause gave the sentries and possibly reinforcements hastening to their aid time to recover. As Mosby's column surged into motion again, rifle fire resounded in the night, the muzzle flashes creating discordant patterns of light on both sides of the road.

It didn't even occur to Chamberlain to draw his pistol and shoot back, but some of Mosby's men fired at the muzzle flashes as they rode. "Cease fire!" Mosby commanded. "You're just giving them targets and telling the entire countryside where we are! Keep moving and keep as quiet as you can!"

Chamberlain remembered the rest of that night as a series of darkened roads, occasional unlit buildings rushing past, the world silent except for the rattle of harness and wagons and the thud of horse hooves upon the dirt or wooden or macadamized road surfaces they crossed. He grew increasingly weary, having no idea where they were, just following Mosby's guides as they rode ahead, and listening to the occasional bursts of sounds in the distance which marked pursuers searching for them. Once, distant volleys of gunfire brought a tired chuckle from a man riding near Chamberlain. "They think they're shooting at us," the man explained. "Wonder who they're really throwing lead at?"

Dawn found them in a heavily-wooded area, on a deeply-rutted track barely wide enough for the wagons, going up and down an apparently endless series of ridges. Everyone was walking now, leading horses as tired as the men who had ridden them. As Chamberlain trudged onward, Mosby came up beside him, looking grim enough to rouse Chamberlain from his fatigue-induced daze. "Is something wrong, colonel?"

Mosby exhaled heavily, his own visage haggard with weariness. "Almost perfect, professor. Almost perfect. But those regulars at the second checkpoint who fired upon us ruined the score."

"They hit someone?"

"Several someones. The wagons made perfect targets. One of the men we freed is dead, and several others wounded." Mosby rubbed his forehead with his free hand. "Lincoln is one of the wounded. In the leg. We've a man with some small medical experience with us, and he's done what he can, but we need to get Lincoln to a decent surgeon soon or we'll likely lose him. There's a town we can go through up ahead where we have a lot of support. Pray to God, sir, that their surgeon can save Lincoln."

**LONGSTREET SAT DOWN,** looking even gloomier than usual. "He'll live."

The dissonance between Longstreet's appearance and his news momentarily confused Chamberlain and the others, then Hancock laughed. "Do you have any more bad news, James?"

"Yeah, Win, I do." Longstreet rubbed his head with both hands. "He can't walk, can't ride. Not for some time. We'll need to transport him by wagon, and we can't move too fast or over roads too rough."

"That is bad news," Hancock agreed. "How long can we let Lincoln rest here before we move?"

Mosby came in just then and shook his head. "Not another day. Our attack on Fortress Monroe has stirred the giant to action. Scouts are reporting the federals are mustering strong forces at a dozen points around my territory. They mean to quarter this region, find Lincoln, and do as much damage to my forces as they can. We need to get Lincoln out before the neck of the bag is tightened." Dropping a map onto the table, he spread it out, then beckoned to Hancock. "You are still resolved to lead the escort for Lincoln?"

"Yes, colonel," Hancock replied.

"The further we get from my area the less I know of the roads, but this map is supposed to be a decent one." Mosby's finger moved as he indicated a route. "You have two advantages. They do not yet know our full strength and may underestimate how much we can send with you, and they do not yet know that Lincoln was hurt, so they are going to assume we will try to move him out by going due west or northwest and avoiding good roads. That means they will not have as much guarding the decent roads and will not be expecting a move through the relatively open country to the north, so if you are strong enough you will be able to break through any pickets and keep going."

Longstreet snorted. "Once they figure out what we're doing and in what strength that advantage will not last."

"No, it will not," Mosby agreed. "You will have to move as fast as the roads and Lincoln's condition permit. Take the best roads north, cut through Maryland and into Pennsylvania, then angle west. If what Captain Longstreet says is true, and we have no reason to doubt him, the closer to Illinois you get the more likely that the local populace will spring to your aid when they learn you are escorting Lincoln home. Get through Pennsylvania to Ohio and, though you will still face federal sympathizers and military forces, you will probably be through the worst of it and picking up new volunteers every mile you go."

"What can you give me to get that far?" Hancock asked.

"I am going to be under a lot of pressure from those federal columns searching for Lincoln and seeking revenge for our raid on Fort Monroe. We stuck a stick into a hornet's nest there. That's fine. It couldn't be helped."

Hancock was studying the map. "Hell. You can't give me enough cavalry to get through, can you?"

"No. I'll give you a company's worth. One hundred men. Captain Buford will join us here tonight and will be in command of your cavalry."

That brought a grin to Hancock's face. "I couldn't ask for a better damned cavalryman. How much leg infantry?"

"Two hundred fifty. That's more than I can spare, but infantry won't do me much good evading federal hunters around here and

I don't think I will be able to manage any stand up fights." Mosby straightened, his eyes still on the map. "And six wagons. At the pace you will have to maintain some will break down on the way, so I'm giving you more than you need."

"In the final throw, we're just going to need one," Armistead commented. "One to carry Lincoln."

Mosby looked at Armistead. "We? You wish to go with Hancock? He will also have Longstreet and Buford, of course."

"If he will have me."

Hancock laughed. "I wouldn't go to the dance without you, Lo."

Chamberlain stood up. "Major Hancock—"

"Colonel," Hancock corrected, indicating his rank insignia. "The Army of the New Republic needs more colonels, and everyone seemed to think I qualified. Damned if I know why."

"The rest of us know," Longstreet mumbled. "You're a good soldier, Win."

"Colonel Hancock," Chamberlain began again. "May I accompany your force as well?"

"Volunteering again, professor?" Hancock smiled derisively. "The old soldiers here will tell you that's a damned dangerous habit."

"But will you have me, sir? I can follow orders."

"Stop toying with him, Win," Armistead said. "Colonel Mosby said Chamberlain did a creditable job during the raid on Fortress Monroe."

"That he did! Facing down Bobbie Lee in full wrath is the act of a damned brave man or a damned fool!" Hancock looked to Mosby. "Can you spare the professor, colonel?"

Mosby nodded. "Make what use you can of him, sir. He displayed a level head and cool courage during the raid. I commend his abilities to you, Colonel Hancock."

Hancock raised his eyebrows. "Professor, you have just received high praise. If Lo and Colonel Mosby vouch for you, I'll be happy to have you along. I hope you enjoy walking. There's going to be a lot of it."

**FORTUNATELY FOR THE** column under Hancock's command, Mosby's assessment had proven accurate. Marching as quickly as they could while burdened with wagons and wounded, the volunteers of the Army of the New Republic brushed aside a series of relatively weak roadblocks. In only one case did they have to fight their way through a checkpoint. At all others the outnumbered federals were easily put to flight or overwhelmed by sudden attacks in the dead of the night. Hancock's forces moved steadily through Virginia and up through Maryland, actually tending east of north at times to stay on the good roads. They had made it into areas less heavily-wooded, with more farms and orchards filling the rolling landscape, as well as towns and villages with homes built of brick, stone or wood lining the road. The area felt quiet, peaceful, the marching column of soldiers and their wagons an alien presence among the farms and other gentle pursuits of this region.

Chamberlain would have been cheered by the success thus far but for two things; the ever grimmer expressions on the professional soldiers which told him they did not expect the good fortune to last, and the pain in his feet and legs from long marches each day with as few rest breaks as possible. Even the mounted soldiers were drooping with weariness as they alternated riding and leading their horses in order to avoid wearing out their mounts. Chamberlain, still wearing the officer's cavalry hat given him for the raid on Fortress Monroe, was grateful for its protection when the sun beat down on the marching volunteers. He was less grateful as the miles wore on for the weight of the revolver hanging from his belt, not only because of its physical burden but because it served as a constant reminder that he might soon be forced to fire that weapon at other men.

One of the things that kept Chamberlain going was the fact that when Armistead wasn't riding or walking with his old friend Hancock, he usually walked beside Chamberlain, the older man showing an endurance that the college professor envied. They spoke of many things as the days passed, including the message which Lee had given Chamberlain at Fort Monroe. "He meant it sincerely," Armistead sighed, "but Bobbie Lee has blinded himself to what he serves. He feels duty and honor leave him no option, and so he does what he must."

"I tried to reason with him."

"I don't expect he listened. Such a decision is a deeply personal thing. And, of course, Colonel Lee is a wealthy landowner, his estates just south of Washington. To choose to join us would be to choose to turn his back on all he owns."

"Including his negro slaves," Chamberlain said.

"There is that, and fear of what those slaves might do if freed. It's like holding a tiger by the tail. They feel they must hold the slaves in check for fear of the consequences of letting go."

"And yet this tiger is of their own making, and endures to this day by their own choice."

Armistead shook his head. "I will not argue the virtues of slavery. Certainly those who were willing to hold the negroes in bondage all too easily proved willing to hold the country in bondage as well. But if eliminating this thing were easily done, surely it would have been done before this by those greater than us. Now we must face it, because those who hold the slaves also would hold us. Deciding what to do is a personal Rubicon we all must come to, Professor Chamberlain. Some of us will have great difficulty deciding whether or not to cross, others will find the decision an easy one."

"It's an apt metaphor." Chamberlain looked out over the countryside, green fields, orchards, a fine land and people at least technically at peace until now. "Are you sorry you crossed the Rubicon, Captain Armistead?"

He shook his head again. "I deeply regret the necessity, but I am content I chose this path, though it pains me to think of the former comrades I may now face in battle, and of those who will call me traitor to my home and my people. Colonel Lee offered me another road. I chose not to pursue his offer, though sometimes I think my decision wavered on a sword's edge, and could have fallen the other way, so that I would have had to dread facing Win Hancock in battle."

"Could you have done that? I've known the two of you but a short time, and yet even I can see how close you are to each other."

"If things had been different…" Armistead's voice trailed off and he walked silently alongside Chamberlain for a long time.

Chamberlain also looked in on Lincoln at times, worried by the suffering evident on the man whose person and words would mean so much. Weak from his wound, the lawyer from Illinois spent much of each day barely conscious as he lay upon blankets in the bed of a wagon, shielded from the direct rays of the sun by the wagon's cover. On one occasion, when Lincoln had been awakened to drink water drawn from a well the column had stopped at, the homely man gazed intently at Chamberlain. "Professor Chamberlain, why are you here?"

Chamberlain was not accustomed to being lost for words, but now he fumbled for an answer. "It is on my way home."

"Surely there are many paths to your home which do not involve the implements of war," Lincoln observed.

"There are," Chamberlain agreed. "But I must do something for liberty, for the safety and freedom of others. I cannot think only of what is best for me."

A weak smile showed on Lincoln's gaunt face. "Do you know why I hate slavery so, Professor Chamberlain? It is not only the terrible suffering it causes those who are slaves, not only the harm it does our Republic, but also because I have seen how it affects those who are not slaves. How it causes the real friends of freedom in the world to doubt our sincerity, and especially because it forces so many really good men amongst ourselves into an open war with the very fundamental principles of civil liberty, insisting there is no right principle of action but *self-interest*."

Chamberlain shook his head, preparing to step down from the wagon where Lincoln lay as the column prepared to begin marching once more. "I cannot accept injustice done to others any more than I can accept it done to myself."

"In that simple proposition rests the hope for the future of all mankind," Lincoln said in a weak voice as Chamberlain dropped back onto the dusty road and slogged wearily in the wake of the wagon.

They finally entered Pennsylvania. The next day, as the column marched north along a route known as the Taneytown road, minor heights rose on their left, thickly wooded hills merging into a long ridge which paralleled the road. Up ahead, Chamberlain could see where the ridge once again became a series of hills whose slopes merged, the hills bending to the east to run perpendicular to the Taneytown road as it reached them and then on a small distance more before ending in a wide gap before some more heights rose farther to the east. As he studied the hills ahead, Chamberlain realized that another substantial road approached those same heights from his right, coming in at an angle from the southeast until it climbed the hills not far to the right of the Taneytown road.

Captain Buford came riding by and Chamberlain hailed him. "Captain, do you know what that road is?"

Buford looked to the right and nodded. "The Baltimore Pike, sir. If any federal forces are moving against us they may well be coming up that road. We're not that far from Baltimore and its regular army garrison. My scouts have seen no sign of any regulars as of yet, but this isn't the west where you can see to the horizon in every direction."

"I heard that you'd been in the west."

"Yes." Buford's eyes went distant with memories. "Campaigning against the plains Indians as well as the Texicans. There's some tough foes for you. They taught me a few lessons. Between them and Colonel Mosby I've picked up some new ways of fighting of which the regular army would never approve." He nodded ahead. "There's a town just over those heights. We may get news there, and Colonel Hancock means to give the men and horses a respite."

It was not yet noon when they reached the hill lying across the road. On the right near the bottom of the hill a farmhouse sat silent, worried faces peering from its windows as the volunteers went by. The slope up the side of the hill was gentle but long, the weary men of the column struggling to reach the crest. When they finally reached the top, Colonel Hancock held up his hand. "Column halt! Captain Buford, please send some of your mounted men into town to buy us some provisions and to see what the townsfolk can tell us. Everyone else fall out and get some rest."

The volunteers flopped down, exhausted, some laying wherever they had stopped and others making their way to the shade of a cluster of trees on the west side of the road. Despite his own tiredness, Chamberlain walked a few more steps to survey the landscape.

On the other side of the hill, buildings clustered about a quarter of a mile to the north around the area where the Taneytown road, the Baltimore Pike, and a third road coming up from the southwest joined or ran close together into the town. From the height, Chamberlain could see at least a half dozen more roads branching out from the town toward the north, east, west and cardinal directions in between, as well as a rail line running into the town from the east and unfinished work on the same line continuing to the west.

Continuing his survey, Chamberlain saw a series of ridges running away to the northwest like great serried swells on the surface of a green and rocky sea. The land appeared to be fairly flat and open to the northeast. Where he stood the Taneytown road passed between a cluster of trees on the west and an open field to the east with just a few trees dotting it. Perhaps a quarter-mile to the east where the Baltimore Pike also crested the hill Chamberlain could see a tall brick structure with a center opening shaped like an arch. Clustered near the side of the brick building facing Chamberlain were the shapes of tombstones and memorials. He couldn't help wondering if the presence of a cemetery on the hill was an omen.

Turning all the way around, he stared southeast to where the Baltimore Pike disappeared between forested heights a few miles distant.

Captain Longstreet, his expression somber, came up beside Chamberlain. "Good ground," Longstreet observed. "If a man had to fight a battle, there would be many worse places to defend than this."

"You wouldn't want to attack here?" Chamberlain asked.

"No, sir, I would not. Good high ground to entrench your troops and artillery and observe the enemy's movement, a series of ridges defenders could fall back upon, and good clear fields of fire." Longstreet shook his head. "But soldiers are rarely allowed to chose their battlefields. A man fights where he must, and when he must." Longstreet bent a searching gaze on Chamberlain. "Do you know when you will fight, sir?"

"When I must, I suppose."

"Will you stand your ground then? Or seek safety?"

Chamberlain gazed into the distance. "I hope I stand with my friends, captain. I hope I stand with those things I believe in. Does any man know the answer for certain before he faces that situation?"

"No." Longstreet blew out a long breath. "I was wounded at Chapultepec, professor, standing with my friends. I have served my country loyally and well."

"You are still serving it well, if my opinion matters, captain."

"Opinions will vary, professor." Longstreet looked around again. "Good ground." Then he walked heavily away, leaving Chamberlain still staring down the Baltimore Pike.

They had been resting for only perhaps half an hour and Buford's men had just delivered provisions acquired in the town when a scout rode over to the officers, rendering a swift and sloppy salute. "There's a rider coming up the pike from Baltimore. He's in a hurry."

Hancock came to stand beside Armistead and Chamberlain, watching the approaching rider with concerned eyes. "One of ours?" he asked Buford.

"He's in regular army uniform," Buford reported, lowering his field glasses. "A courier, maybe. We'll stop him." He beckoned to several of his soldiers, who mounted up and rode down to meet the horseman.

They could see the lone horseman ride steadily to meet Buford's men, join up with them, and after a brief talk the entire group came up the road.

The rider's horse was covered with foam, its tongue lolling out as the rider dismounted with a stagger. "Captain Buford, is he here?"

"Here, soldier."

The man saw Buford and even through the dust and sweat coating his face the others could see it brighten. He straightened to attention and saluted. "I served under you, sir, out west."

Buford eyed him, then smiled and nodded. "Corporal Jenkins."

"Yes, sir." The corporal's own smile vanished as quickly as it had come. "I have deserted from my unit, sir."

"So have we all," Buford replied.

The soldier grinned with relief. "I wish to join you. I have important news."

"Very well, corporal. You are welcome. Make your report."

The familiar ritual seemed to steady the exhausted soldier, who stood without wavering and recited his information clearly. "Sir, there is a force under Colonel Lee in pursuit of you. My company was attached to the Baltimore garrison, but more cavalry and infantry along with Colonel Lee came up the Chesapeake by ship a couple of days ago and we all headed out. The column is proceeding up the Baltimore Pike and consists of a regiment of infantry and two companies of cavalry. I left it about ten miles back when I had a chance to get off unseen as they stopped to rest in a town. They know this town here is where many roads converge. They're pushing on fast and hoped to get here before you did, so as to cut you off."

"Ten miles." Hancock spat out a lurid curse. "Too damned close."

"Who's in command of the cavalry?" Buford asked.

"Captain Stuart, sir."

"Stuart? J.E.B. Stuart?"

"Yes, sir."

Buford nodded heavily, then looked toward Hancock. "I know how to handle Stuart."

"Do you? He's a good cavalryman, I've heard."

"Good enough," Buford conceded. "Very good. But he's also predictable in some ways. He wants to be seen by everyone as the best. As a cavalryman, he believes in great charges, fighting saber to saber from the saddle. He's good at that, so we don't want to fight his battle." Buford studied the terrain, his eyes narrowing. "Will we try to delay them?"

"We have to," Hancock replied. "The question is where."

"Here," Longstreet stated bluntly. "It's as strong a position as you'll find, and the men and horses need time to rest before a fight. If you push on now Stuart's cavalry may catch our entire force with man and beast at the end of their strength."

Hancock pursed his mouth, looking downward, then nodded. "We have enough with us to stop Lee here."

"If what is with Lee is all that he has," Buford pointed out. "Corporal, do you know whether or not any other regular columns are converging on this area?"

The cavalry corporal shook his head, looking regretful. "No, sir. I don't know if there's more units in the area or where they're going."

"My scouts haven't the time or the numbers to know the answer," Buford admitted. "But a crossroads like this, along the route they must by now have realized we are taking, is a logical place for Lee to concentrate his forces."

Longstreet grimaced. "The best place to make a stand, but the worst one as well. We could have columns as strong as Lee's coming from the north, east and from the south in pursuit of us. If we all stay here, we may all be trapped here, or at the least face attacking forces from more than one direction. But if we all push on, Bobbie Lee will catch us for certain."

Hancock seemed to be chewing over Longstreet's words, then spat. "Damn. I don't want you to be right, James, but you might be. You're advising that I leave part of this force to delay Lee and push the rest on to the northwest to avoid any other columns converging on this place."

"I am, sir. It's not a hopeless battle for those left here. It's not hard to predict what the enemy will do." Longstreet pointed down the pike. "You know Bobbie Lee. He'll march his infantry right up the road with an eye to smashing through any blocking force here, and send his cavalry around those hills to the east to get behind the blocking force and trap it so it gets hit from both front and back. Textbook solution. I'll be ready for it. With this ground I believe I can throw Lee back, and then withdraw and rejoin the rest of you before any regular army reinforcements get here."

"No, sir," Hancock replied, shaking his head. "Not you, James. We need you when we get to Indiana and Illinois. You know the Army of the New Republic people in those states and you know the states themselves."

Longstreet seemed disposed to argue, but Buford spoke up. "The blocking force will require my cavalry, so I need to remain.

I'll draw the regular cavalry into a fight in the town where its numbers won't matter. Stuart won't be able to resist trying to fight my mounted troops, and once he starts fighting them he'll stay tied down and never mind any orders to do otherwise."

"Are you certain?" Hancock asked.

"I'm betting my life on it," Buford responded dryly, then something else seemed to occur to him and he turned back to the corporal. "Two companies of cavalry, you said. Who's with Stuart? What other cavalry officers are with that force?"

"Just a young fool named Custer in charge of the other company, sir." The corporal looked aghast at his candor. "Begging your pardon, sir."

"That's all right, corporal," Buford assured him. He glanced at Hancock. "From what I hear, that's an apt description of Custer. Last in his class at the Point. Headstrong, impulsive, and very political. Small wonder he made captain so quickly, and he'll badly want a glorious victory here to boost his chances at promotion to major. Custer won't offer any wise counsel, even if Stuart were willing to listen, and since he's junior to Stuart he has to follow Stuart's orders."

"Good." Hancock indicated the Baltimore Pike. "Corporal, you said Lee is in command of the column, but who's in command of the infantry regiment?"

The corporal bit his lip, plainly thinking. "A Major...Scythes?"

"Scythes? There's no—Sickles. Is it Major Sickles?"

"Yes, sir! That's it, sir! Sickles."

"A politician of dubious military merit earning his credit for service. Lee and Stuart are capable officers, but otherwise we've some luck in our opponents, it seems." Hancock looked around

slowly, eyeing the terrain and his forces on the hill, then nodded. "Very well, Captain Buford. I'll give you all but twenty of
our mounted men. I need to keep some for scouts and couriers.
But you can't command the defense against Lee's infantry coming
up the pike if you're overseeing dealing with Lee's cavalry in the
town. We need an officer to be in charge of the infantry blocking
force." Hancock's words came out reluctantly, then he turned a
grim look on Armistead.

Armistead nodded calmly. "I'm the only one left, Win. It's not
like you have a choice."

"Damn it all, I know you can do it. Captain Armistead, what
would you need to hold your position?"

"Everything we've got and then some." Armistead smiled
crookedly. "But give me what you can, Win, and I'll make do."

Hancock pivoted back to face the rider. "Corporal, is Major
Sickle's infantry regiment at full strength?"

"No, sir," the corporal replied immediately. "Ain't no unit at
full strength, these days. He's got about four hundred infantry,
maybe five hundred."

Hancock chewed his lip, staring at the grass again, then
looked at Armistead. "Can you hold him with fifty men?"

Armistead pursed his lips and gazed down the pike as if
Lee's regiment were already visible, then eastward toward where
the road came up the hill near the cemetery. "I've seen worse
defensive positions, but ten to one odds isn't recommended in
the textbooks, Win."

"I'm not asking you to kick Bobbie Lee's ass back to
Baltimore, Lo. Just hold here a while. We can't travel near as

fast as we'd like with Lincoln hurt and everyone exhausted. Give us time to put some distance between us and that damned regular army column, then you and Buford's men are to come on fast and rejoin us before any more regular columns come from other directions. But I've got to keep a strong force with me in case we run into more regulars on Chambersburg Pike. If we do, James Longstreet and I are going to need every man we've got."

"Fifty men?" Armistead saluted. "Yes, sir. Request permission to ask for volunteers."

"Do so, sir."

"Sergeant Maines, form the men. We have little time," Hancock directed. "Choose the volunteers quickly and then release the rest so we can prepare to move out as quickly as possible."

As they waited for the men with them to fall into formation, Chamberlain stepped close to Armistead. "Captain, I have a request to make."

"Then please do so, sir. We are a little pressed for time."

"I know how important this is. I...would like to volunteer to be part of your command. If that is the right way to say it."

Armistead smiled. "Close enough, sir. Your offer is accepted." He looked at Hancock, who had been glowering into the distance but now smiled back briefly as if both men were sharing a private joke.

The fifty volunteers were selected and forming up when Longstreet rode over to where Armistead and Chamberlain stood. "You're staying, professor?"

Chamberlain nodded. "I found my Rubicon."

"Have you? Don't let down the men fighting beside you, professor." Longstreet turned a somber gaze on Armistead. "Things have changed since Mexico, Lo. You know that. A lot of people don't. They think it's still about marching troops in tight formations straight at the enemy and trading volleys at close range. But it's not smooth-bore muskets anymore. There are rifles now. Breech-loading carbines, even repeaters. One man under cover can hold off a dozen."

"There's truth to that," Armistead agreed.

"Most of your men have weapons they don't need to load standing up. Keep them spread out, shooting from behind any cover they can find. That's my advice. Damn, Lo. I want to stay and do this myself. It's my fault we're here." Longstreet frowned toward the south. "I don't like it, Lo. Fighting Bobbie Lee. Helluva thing."

"We have all chosen this, James. I am not happy about it, either. I pray that God has given me the wisdom to make the right choice, and that He have mercy on us all no matter our choice."

"Hmph." Longstreet turned his horse with a final look southward. "There's no mercy in this world or the next, Lo. All that awaits us is whatever destinies our choices dictate. Good luck."

"Good luck, James."

As Longstreet rode off, Hancock returned, also mounted, looking so magnificent that Chamberlain finally fully understood why he had heard Hancock referred to as 'the superb' by some of the men. Hancock sat in his saddle, looking south. "Lo, your orders are to hold Bobbie Lee. Hold him until sunset if possible, but not longer than that. You are to withdraw and follow us after sunset, establishing any further blocking positions as you deem necessary given the state of your command and the situation regarding the enemy. Don't worry about Buford. If anyone can tie down the regular cavalry, it's him. Just coordinate your movements with Buford and all should be well." Hancock turned his eyes on Armistead. "I wish I could leave you more men. There will be a lot of pressure on you."

"We will give you the time you need, Win," Armistead assured him.

"As God is my witness, I wish I could stay here and fight beside you."

"You have your own responsibilities and you're a good enough officer to know that. In any event, you will be here in spirit, and by the Lord's grace we're on the same side," Armistead replied with a smile.

Hancock grimaced, then speared Chamberlain with his gaze. "What of you, professor? You have volunteered to fight here, and Captain Armistead could use help in commanding the defense of this position."

"Commanding?" Chamberlain looked from Hancock to Armistead in surprise. "I'm no West Point man, sir."

"Neither is Mosby. I've been watching and listening to you, and you've skill despite your lack of training, an understanding of the difference between theory and action which many an armchair warrior lacks." Hancock nodded grimly to Chamberlain. "And unless my instincts are wrong, sir, you are a leader men will follow. Will you accept a field commission and serve as Major Armistead's deputy?"

"Major?" Armistead asked.

"A field promotion, Lo. I just decided on it. It's not right I should be a colonel and you a captain. Would you be right with Chamberlain as a deputy?"

"I would."

Chamberlain swallowed, thinking of the regular army column marching toward this location. He knew too much history to believe that victory here would be easy or inevitable. Far from it. Hancock clearly hated to leave his friend Armistead here, but both men understood the need.

As did he, Chamberlain realized. Words meant nothing if men were not willing to personally sacrifice for the principles in which they believed. He took a deep breath and faced Hancock. "Yes, sir. I would be honored to accept a field commission."

"Then raise your right hand, sir. Do you swear to serve faithfully in the Army of the New Republic, to uphold and defend the Constitution of the United States of America against all enemies foreign and domestic and to follow all lawful orders given you by those officers senior to you in authority?"

"I do, sir."

"Then I hereby appoint you to the brevet rank of captain of volunteers in the Army of the New Republic. Do your duty, sir." Hancock seized his reins and made to turn his horse's head, then paused for another look at Armistead. "Farewell, Lo."

"Farewell," Armistead echoed, saluting.

Hancock returned the salute, then pulled his horse around and galloped down the road toward where the rest of the column had begun moving steadily away.

Armistead spent a moment watching Hancock, then shifted his appraisal to the men awaiting his commands. "Let's get the troops over to the other side of the hill and make sure they are properly placed, Captain Chamberlain. We have some rifles and some carbines, but also a fair number of pistols and shotguns. We will need to let the attackers get close before we fire, and that means getting the troops under cover as Captain Longstreet advised. There is little time nor tools to dig trenches, but we will do what we can."

"Yes, sir." Chamberlain saluted. "May I ask you something?"

"Of course."

"You didn't seem surprised when Colonel Hancock proposed me as your deputy."

Armistead smiled at Chamberlain. "Win and I both knew that you had already joined us in your heart, sir. He also spoke truly in his assessment of you. You will need confidence in yourself this day. Lack that confidence, and the men will know. Believe that what Colonel Hancock said of you is true, and together we will hold this hill. There goes the wagon with Mr. Lincoln. If you wish any farewells with him, you had best do so now."

Chamberlain ran over to the wagon, which had just started to move, and pulled himself up onto the back. Inside he saw Lincoln lying on his pile of blankets, the plain-featured face drawn with strain and suffering from the wound and the rough travel. With no opportunity for shaving, a beard had begun sprouting on Lincoln's chin, but the growth did not further roughen the man's features, instead lending him some extra measure of dignity. "I'm staying here, Mr. Lincoln, with the soldiers who will be holding off the regulars. I just wanted to say goodbye."

"Goodbye, Professor Chamberlain, and thank you for all you have done." Lincoln offered his hand, which Chamberlain was relieved to find cool and not hot with fever.

"It is Captain Chamberlain now," he advised Lincoln.

Lincoln smiled with surprising gentleness. "I hope to be worthy of the men who are defending me, Captain Chamberlain. Will I see you in Illinois?"

"Perhaps." Chamberlain didn't know if he would ever leave this hill, but he didn't want to speak of that. "Events are coming to a head, it seems. I need to return to Maine, to help raise the state in rebellion in support of the New Republic, and then raise soldiers to help the struggle in other states."

"A difficult and worthy labor, captain. My good wishes go with you."

"There is little I can do, Mr. Lincoln, compared to what you can do. A man of the people must lead this rebellion against those who hold the people and the Republic in slavery."

"You do me too much honor, sir." Lincoln smiled, though sadness held his eyes as if they could see a future which held much sorrow and loss. "I will gather the forces of liberty and direct them as best I may, though I will be much like the man riding a river in flood on a raft, who seeks first to keep the raft afloat as the raging flood goes where it will. But perhaps this flood can be guided along a better course."

"I'll help all that I can, sir." Chamberlain dropped off the wagon, watching it go, then jogged back to where Armistead waited.

As they led the fifty volunteers east to where the Baltimore Pike climbed up the side of the ridge near the cemetery, Captain

Buford rode by and saluted Armistead. "I'll keep Stuart busy, Lo. See you at sunset." Then Buford led his column of mounted troops down into the town, where the residents, having seen the preparations for battle, had vanished from the streets.

When Chamberlain reached the Baltimore Pike he saw that the arch of the brick gateway to the cemetery faced it from just off the road. Most of the windows in the building also faced the road, with only one looking down the pike. "Pity," Armistead muttered. "That could have been a useful defensive position." Aside from a few trees and the grave markers and memorials there was little other cover on the west side of the pike.

On the east side of the pike the hill rose a bit farther, its top almost clear of trees except for a copse near the eastern side away from the pike. Farmers' fields occupied this side of the pike, and a series of low walls made of carefully piled stone ran perpendicular to the pike, the nearest such wall almost even with the cemetery gatehouse and just short of the crest of the hill. The slope up the pike here to the top of the hill was significantly shorter and steeper than where the Taneytown road came up to the west, especially on the side of the pike where the cemetery lay.

"Sergeant Maines," Armistead ordered. "A cemetery will have shovels at hand. Get them. Inform the owners, if they are about, that we will either return the shovels or leave adequate compensation." Armistead moved his arm, pointing. "I will place half the men on each side of the pike. Two on the east side can fight from the gate house but the rest must dig and throw up such bastions as they can manage in the time we have. The troops on the west side of the road will fight from behind the stone wall and dig what trenches they may in its lee to improve their own cover."

Maines saluted. "Yes, sir."

"The men must not be worn out when the regulars arrive, sergeant. We need to pace their work at fortifying this area."

"Yes, sir. I'll go acquire the shovels, sir."

"Captain Chamberlain," Armistead said as the sergeant left, "supervise the men digging in behind the stone wall. Make sure they are spread out, but that we have good strength toward the pike and are prepared to strike from the flank any force trying to charge past us up the road."

"Yes, sir. How do I do that?"

Armistead smiled for a moment, then he used his hands to emphasize his words. "Throw up some of the dirt from the digging so it forms a bastion at the corner of the wall where it meets the road. Have it form a position from which several men can fire directly at the road and be protected, while also blocking anyone on the road from firing down the wall at the men behind it."

Chamberlain found to his surprise that the men followed his directions without protest. The sun swung across the sky as the defenders labored to improve the natural defenses for the hill, everyone stealing glances down the Baltimore Pike whenever they took a break. Finally one man called out as five of Buford's scouts came into view, tearing down the pike, but veering off toward the gap to the east well before reaching the slope leading up the hill. Behind them came at least twenty regular cavalrymen in pursuit, all of them following Buford's men toward the gap.

Armistead brought out field glasses, standing in the center of the pike looking south, appearing totally calm. "The rest of the cavalry is in sight," he told Chamberlain. "They are heading straight for the gap to the east of us, where Buford is waiting for them." A flurry of shots sounded in that direction. "And where Captain Buford has just shown his command in full view and greeted the regular cavalry vanguard who forgot in the thrill of the chase their duty to screen the advance of their comrades."

Chamberlain looked to the east, seeing several surviving cavalrymen retreating at high speed back to the south, then had his attention brought back to the pike by Armistead. "The infantry is in sight. They're marching in good form. Either the corporal forgot to mention it or Colonel Lee has already received reinforcements. There are two cannon accompanying Lee's force. Light horse artillery, but it can't be discounted."

"Does it look like five hundred infantry?" Chamberlain asked.

"Very like that," Armistead confirmed, pivoting to study the situation to the southeast. "It appears all of the regular cavalry is heading for the gap and the town. John Buford is going to have his hands full." Then Armistead sighed sadly, surprising Chamberlain. "There's Stuart. It's got to be him. I never thought to be fighting against Lee and Stuart as well. Bad enough to be fighting the United States Army, but to have it led by those I once served beside makes it worse."

Chamberlain and Armistead stood there in the road, while the regular infantry marched closer, Chamberlain feeling ridiculously exposed. "Do you think when they see us here they will move west and come up the Taneytown road as we did?" Chamberlain asked.

Armistead shook his head. "No, sir. I do not consider it likely. Colonel Lee's first move will certainly be an attempt to sweep us aside with as little delay as possible. Marching across the fields toward the Taneytown road will take time, and we could easily shift our own frontage to meet him there since we would have far less ground to cover. Regular forces also tend to have contemptuous attitudes toward volunteers. That and Lee's need for speed will work against a flanking maneuver with his infantry. He will come straight at us."

A farmhouse stood perhaps a quarter mile down the pike on the east side of the road, and as Chamberlain watched the regulars marched even with the farmhouse, then came to a halt. The two cannon stopped behind them but the men riding the caissons made no moves to unlimber the guns. Another roar of gunfire arose to the northeast, this time tapering off into sustained shooting punctuating the blare of bugles. Armistead, his field glasses to his eyes again, shook his head. "Stuart's companies are sounding the charge, just as Buford predicted. They're charging into the town, while Buford's men are dismounting and taking up positions behind cover and in houses. Stuart is going to try to defeat Buford's force on Buford's chosen ground, but Buford won't oblige him with a traditional cavalry fight. Stuart has blundered, but he and Lee have also both just made a more serious error."

"What's that?"

"Stuart's cavalry could have felt out our numbers and our positions, then the cavalry could have galloped to the Taneytown road and up it while Lee's infantry held us pinned here. Neither Lee nor Stuart wants to take the time needed to reconnoiter us, and so they have to assume we have someone blocking the Taneytown road as well. But because they rushed to battle before scouting out our positions, their cavalry is now tied down fighting in a place they didn't expect to encounter resistance and they know nothing of our positions on this hill." Armistead lowered his field glasses. "Always try to learn as much about the enemy as you can *before* you make your plans, Captain Chamberlain."

"I will remember that, sir."

"See that you do. That is what Hancock, Longstreet, Buford and you and I did. You would be surprised how many professionals fail to recall the necessity of taking the enemy into account before they decide on a course of action, though."

The infantry on the road stood in ranks in the hot sun, waiting. Chamberlain could see officers on horseback riding up to each other, possibly discussing the gunfire being heard from over the hill where Buford was tying down Stuart. He was peering at them as if that would allow him to discern their intentions when Sergeant Maines spoke behind him. "Begging your pardon, Major Armistead and Captain Chamberlain, but we have another volunteer."

Chamberlain turned along with Armistead, seeing an elderly man clasping a vintage musket in one hand. The man came to attention and saluted. "Private John Burns, reporting for duty, sir."

Armistead returned the salute solemnly. "You appear to have fought your battles long before this, sir."

"I fought against tyranny in the War of 1812 and I can fight against it now. I have no horse, but your cavalry captain suggested you could use reinforcements here on Cemetery Hill."

Burns must have read the hesitation in Armistead. "I have seen seventy years on this earth, sir. I do not fear dying now in the cause of liberty."

"Then take your position in the line, sir," Armistead ordered, waving Burns toward the positions occupied by the defenders on the west side of the road. "Inside the gate house. Fire from the window along with the men already there."

"Yes, sir." With another salute, the old man marched behind Sergeant Maines toward the gate house.

Armistead caught Chamberlain's look. "He has spirit, captain. A vital element in any group of men, but especially important now. These are good men, but they lack enough experience fighting alongside each other, especially against regular troops in force. When Lee begins his attack we must give them simple and clear orders, and ensure they see us during the action. Do you understand?" His arm raised and swept across the hill top. "They must stay under cover as best they can for protection, but you and I must be seen by them if they are to remain steady. Unfortunately, that means the enemy will see us as well."

Chamberlain managed to smile. "Like Julius Caesar or other Roman generals. They had to lead their legions from the front."

"Exactly, sir." Armistead paused, his eyes on the regulars. "They're on the move. Still in column, but only a company. Surely Colonel Lee would not attempt that, but that is Sickles leading the company. He is rash enough to try such a move without waiting for approval from Lee." Armistead indicated the stone wall to the east of the road. "If you will take up position there, captain, I will command from the right. Wait for my command to fire, and ensure you have enough force at your bastion near the road to hold it against a rush."

His throat suddenly felt very dry, but Chamberlain saluted. "Yes, sir."

He walked over behind the stone wall, but close to it, seeing his men crouched behind the wall and the dirt they had thrown up while digging shallow entrenchments. His men. It didn't feel real at the moment, nor did the steady march of the regulars on the pike, who had now brought their rifles to port arms but were still coming up the pike in a column.

Sergeant Maines walked up beside Chamberlain and shook his head. "It'll be more murder than battle in a moment, captain. Those regulars are going to try to bust through us in column instead of forming a line for fighting."

"Why are they doing it?"

"Because they'll think we'll break at the first blow, sir, and a column makes a fine hammer against light resistance. But if you throw a column against those determined to hold their ground, it is nothing more than a mass of men forming a target a fool could not miss." Sergeant Maines moved along the stone wall, checking to make sure every man was ready to fire.

To Chamberlain, the marching regulars already seemed far too close, an officer riding before them with casual arrogance, not even having bothered to draw either sword or pistol. Now the officer called out. "On the hill! Surrender in the name of the Army of the United States!"

Armistead replied, his voice carrying easily down the slope. "The Army of the New Republic holds this hill, sir, and will hold it in the name of liberty for the people and for the Constitution of the United States of America."

The officer seemed to hesitate, as if surprised to have his order rejected, his horse dancing as its reins were jerked in different directions. Then the mounted officer drew his sword with a dramatic gesture, raising it high as he called out loudly. "Company, advance!"

Armistead's voice came again. "Steady on the left! Steady on the right!"

Chamberlain, his eyes on the officer whose horse was now trotting forward, drew his pistol and echoed Armistead. "Steady!"

"Ready!" Armistead called. Behind the officer, the column of regular soldiers hurried forward, still in tight formation, but slowing as they tackled the slope of the road leading up the hill. "Fire!"

The stone wall before Chamberlain erupted in a blaze of fire and gouts of smoke that momentarily obscured his view of the pike. Amid the chaos of smoke and noise Sergeant Maines kept walking along the wall, ordering the men to continue shooting while Maines himself reloaded his carbine, pausing each time he aimed and fired. Remembering Armistead's orders, Chamberlain forced himself to walk at a steady pace despite legs which threatened to shake uncontrollably, walk to the tiny bastion near the road, where a half-dozen men were firing as fast as they could load.

"Cease fire!" Armistead's command came across the pike, and once again Chamberlain repeated it as the defenders' fire tapered off into a final few shots.

As the smoke blew clear Chamberlain saw that the pike was choked with bodies, blood covering the surface of the road in a dark pool. He wondered what had become of the officer, then saw his horse galloping toward the rear, the regular officer slumped in the saddle. In the officer's wake, the surviving soldiers from the company were running back, but as they encountered the rest of the regiment they were stopped.

Armistead came walking through the smoke, his face impassive. "They will not make that mistake again. Colonel Lee now knows he must fight here, and Major Sickles appears badly enough wounded that he will not be urging any more heedless attacks."

As Armistead had predicted, the next advance revealed a more serious attitude by the regulars toward the defenders. In clear view of the defenders on the hill, but well out of range of any of their weapons, two other companies in the regular regiment marched even with the farm house, then shifted their formations into lines facing the hill. Behind them, the two cannon unlimbered, then began hurling shots toward the defending volunteers. Chamberlain felt an urge to seek cover as the cannon shells began exploding, then realized that the artillery fire was all overshooting, falling behind the defenders' positions. "Them toy guns ain't a problem for us," Sergeant Maines assured the other men behind the wall. "Hitting the top of a hill is hard work even for the best artillerymen. They'll keep dropping rounds on the civilians in the town behind us. You just keep your heads down and aim well when the next attack comes."

Chamberlain got his feet into motion again, walking up and down his short line, trying to act confident as the lines of regular infantry came marching steadily toward the hill. Behind him he could hear sporadic bursts of gunfire and bugle calls where Buford was still tying down Stuart in the streets of the town. If silence fell it would mean Buford had been defeated. It was a surprise to realize that the sounds of combat could be comforting.

The two companies of regular troops had formed up in a straight line, each company's line formation separated from the next by a small gap. Each company line of about one hundred men stood about fifty men long in two ranks, the second close behind the first, each man's shoulders almost touching those of his companions on either side. Officers stood out before their companies, then another officer rode out in front of them all, called a command, and the entire force of regulars began moving up the hill. "How can we miss?" Chamberlain wondered as he looked at them coming steadily closer.

"Not easily," Sergeant Maines observed.

"Why are they attacking like that?"

"By the book, sir. Many a time I've drilled formations in the same way."

It was as Longstreet had said. The regulars were fighting by old rules, even though weapons had changed. But Chamberlain spotted something else that worried him. "The regulars' front is so wide it overlaps ours on each end. Should we spread out our line?"

"That's up to you and Major Armistead, sir," Sergeant Maines deferred.

He thought about asking Armistead, then shook his head. "If we spread out, it will thin our line. I think we need to keep our fire concentrated."

The regulars marched up the slope, maintaining their tight formations, until Armistead called another command. "Riflemen, aim and fire! All others hold fire!"

This time the explosions of fire, noise and smoke took place sporadically along the stone wall and on the other side of the pike among the trees and tombstones. Chamberlain watched as regulars in the oncoming ranks jerked as if they had been punched, knocking backwards to roll a short distance down the slope. The horse of the officer leading the attack reared and fell with an awful scream, but the officer disentangled himself from the stirrups, picked himself up, waved his sword and kept walking.

The long line of regular troops was almost even with the point where the column had been decimated earlier when Armistead gave the order for everyone to open fire. Shotguns, muskets and pistols joined in the barrage. Chamberlain watched as more and more regulars fell, their commander shouting orders which Chamberlain could not make out through the din of gunfire. The regulars halted, raised their rifles to their shoulders and fired in a long rippling volley.

Chamberlain heard the balls from the rifles whipping past, felt the wind from some of them, heard impacts in trees and along the stone wall. A couple of the defenders fell backwards, one yelling in pain. But the others kept firing as the regulars methodically reloaded. This time when the regulars raised their rifles to fire everyone ducked, and Chamberlain stepped behind a tree. The volley tore more holes in living wood and stone, but hit none of the defenders.

Staring through the clouds of powder smoke, Chamberlain wondered why the regulars' lines seemed to be getting shorter.

It finally dawned on him that as soldiers fell, the regulars kept closing up their ranks, shoulder to shoulder, and as a result their lines kept shortening so that now the regulars' formation no longer overlapped the defenders' line. "Why are they doing that?" he shouted to Maines, bewildered. "Closing ranks like that?"

Maines paused to give Chamberlain a puzzled look. "That's what you do, captain. Maintain a tight formation. That's how the regulars drill, that's how they're trained to fight."

Chamberlain got it then. "Like Harold's Saxons at Hastings." Staying close together, providing a tight mass of targets. Eight hundred years separated those regulars from these, yet they were fighting by the same rules.

The officer leading the formation had fallen again at some point, this time not to rise again, but one of the other officers with the regulars came out in front, waved his sword and charged forward, the surviving regular soldiers in the companies running after him to storm the defenders' line.

*Now*, something told Chamberlain. Now he had to stand out and lead from the front as Armistead had advised. Jogging forward to the very edge of the defensive line, his legs touching the low stone wall before him, he shouted over the sound of firing. "Hold them! Keep firing!"

The regulars were very close now, scrambling up the hill, more and more of them falling as the defenders kept firing and both pistols and shotguns took a greater toll on the attackers. Chamberlain drew his own revolver, aimed with a sense of dread and reluctance, then fired for the first time at a living target. He couldn't tell if he had hit the regular, so Chamberlain fired once more, then other regulars were coming close and he fired again and again.

His pistol's hammer clicked on an empty chamber, and Chamberlain realized he couldn't see any more regulars. All along the line, the volunteers were cheering or yelling insults. Gazing through the drifts of smoke, Chamberlain saw the regulars racing down the slope in a mass, their neat formations dissolved into a single clump of humanity. He stood, breathing heavily, his throat painful from the harsh smoke filling the air. Looking down at his pistol, Chamberlain swallowed, then reloaded it with fingers that shook badly. He watched his hands fumbling the bullets into the chambers of the weapon, feeling strangely detached and numb, as if watching someone else far away. Part of him wondered what he would feel when the lack of sensation was replaced by feeling once more.

"Captain Chamberlain!" Someone was calling him from the west side of the pike. Trying to appear calm, something made easier by his temporary emotional removal from everything about him, Chamberlain strolled across the pike, wondering why someone other than Major Armistead had called him.

He found Armistead on the ground, Sergeant Maines kneeling next to him, a dark, wet patch spreading ever larger across the breast of the major's uniform. The sergeant looked up, tears running down his face, as Chamberlain approached. "Took a ball in the chest. He ain't got a chance, sir."

Chamberlain knelt on the other side of Armistead, shocked into feeling again. Major Armistead was taking deep, quivering breaths, each one causing a new swell of blood to well up from the wound in his chest. His eyes met Chamberlains'. "We stopped them again...captain, but...Bobbie Lee will not give up...so easily."

"Yes, sir." He could not think of anything else to say. What did you say to a man dying before you?

"You must...command them, captain." Armistead, his face pale, shuddered again before he could continue speaking. "Take my sword...use it...as a symbol. *Hold* this position, captain."

"I will, sir."

"Hancock...Longstreet...Buford...our country...need us to hold." Armistead coughed up a gout of blood, then shuddered before speaking again. "It is God's will that...I die here, but I thank Him that I have fought my last...alongside Winfield Hancock." His breath rasped as he fought for air and Chamberlain blinked back tears of his own, certain that death was but moments away. But Armistead roused himself once more, focusing on Chamberlain again. "Tell Colonel Hancock... from me...that I have done my duty and...do not doubt the justice of our cause."

"Yes, sir, I will."

Armistead must have heard, because as his last breath sighed from him the old soldier had a contented expression. Sergeant Maines made a low sound of pain as if he had also been shot, then the sergeant picked up Armistead's sword and held out the grip toward Chamberlain.

Moving in a daze, Chamberlain grasped the sword and rose to his feet. Chamberlain looked south to where the regular army forces could be seen forming up near the farmhouse for another attack. His gaze shifted to his own forces and he saw uncertainty and fear rising like a physical fog as word of the major's death raced along the thin line.

"Hold your places there!" Sergeant Maines shouted, running toward where some men were beginning to rise.

The sergeant's curses and discipline would not be enough, Chamberlain knew. He took another look at Armistead, then strode toward the center of the line, onto the Baltimore Pike, raising Armistead's sword high like a banner. Always before this, his speeches had been about theory and ideas. They had not been about convincing men to stand and die at his word. But he knew many such speeches, and now Chamberlain's mind raced from Caesar to Shakespeare to Patrick Henry, trying to craft the words needed to keep these men here.

"Men of the Army of the New Republic!" Chamberlain cried as he came to halt just in front of the line. "Our comrades are depending upon us to hold this hill. We have already thrown back our foes more than once, and we can do it again if we hold to our purpose. I will stand here and fight alone if need be, but if you stand beside me we will achieve a victory which will live in the annals of our history alongside Lexington and Concord, and every man who stands firm on this hill will be remembered forever just as those patriots are today! Not because we held a scrap of ground, but because here we stood up to break the chains of tyranny, to save the Constitution and the liberty bequeathed us by the men who forged this nation. Will you stand with me?"

Sergeant Maines cheered first, but the others joined in, a roar of defiance which caused the regulars below to stare upward at the hill.

For the next attack, the regiment of regulars was formed into a single line, four men deep, but so serious had been the regulars' losses that this line was not as long as that formed earlier by just two companies. Chamberlain walked up and down the stone wall, and across the pike itself as enemy bullets plucked at his clothes, calling out the commands as Armistead had done, standing firm as the regulars charged up so close that they grappled among the tombstones and the stone wall before again falling back.

Chamberlain reloaded his pistol with hands that now shook so badly he could barely hold the shells, stopping when he realized that he had only two cartridges left.

Sergeant Maines, his expression somber, ran up to Chamberlain. "Sir, we're not equipped like regular forces. Not in weapons and not in ammunition. I've checked with the men who are still on their feet and there's not any with more than two shots left, and most of them have but one."

"The regulars have not broken at the first volley in their other attacks."

"No, sir, they have not. But a first volley is all we'll have the next time they come." Maines gazed down through the smoke. "And they are preparing to come again, sir."

"We cannot leave this hill. The others are depending upon us." Chamberlain recited it like a mantra, his own being focused on carrying out Armistead's last command.

"Aye, sir. But we can't stay, neither. We've got, I dunno, ten minutes and then they'll be up and at us again."

What would Armistead do? What would George Washington have done? Chamberlain gazed down at the pistol in his right hand, then his eyes swung to where Armistead's sword was clasped tightly in his left. "Do the men have bayonets?"

"Bayonets?" Maines gave Chamberlain a wondering look. "A few, sir. Everyone's got a knife, and some have got small axes. Tomahawks they call 'em. They used to be standard issue for soldiers."

That made the solution simple enough. Like George Washington at Trenton, outnumbered and desperate, but with a chance to win by attacking when defense no longer held out hope. Chamberlain wondered at the steadiness of his voice as he spoke again. "Sergeant Maines, inform the men that after we fire our next volley I shall give the order to advance. We will…" What was the right term? "Countercharge. We will meet their attack with our own. I will lead the charge down the hill."

"Knives against rifles? You'll lead the way? And them outnumbering us?" The sergeant slowly smiled. "Damn all, sir, that's crazy."

"We are going to do it, sergeant."

"Yes, sir. We sure as hell are, sir. I'll pass the word." Not far off, they could hear commands being shouted as the regulars formed up and began advancing for the fourth time.

Chamberlain, his heart pounding, walked forward until he was near the center of the line, his hands so tight upon pistol and sword that the metal bit painfully into both palms. The regulars were already close, their line smaller than before but still powerful, still deadly even though Chamberlain could tell from their movements how tired the regulars must be. A hard march from Baltimore, then three assaults up the hill, but still they came on a fourth time.

Coming closer up the slope, through the bodies littering the pike and the grass and fields on either side of it, then at shouted orders the regulars broke into a stumbling charge up the hill.

"Steady!" Chamberlain shouted over the crackle of rifle shots as some of the regulars paused to fire. He felt a tug at his shirt as a ball passed close enough to him to rip a hole in the fabric. "Ready!" The regulars reached the line of earlier casualties and kept on, scrambling up the slope, so close that Chamberlain had no trouble seeing their faces. Not just soldiers, not a mass of blue uniforms, but individuals showing their weariness and fear and resolve in eyes and faces.

"Fire!" Chamberlain cried.

The volley erupted from the hilltop, slamming into the regulars and throwing the attack into momentary confusion. "Forward!" Chamberlain shouted as loud as he could. "Charge!" Raising his sword again, and not daring to think about what he was doing, Chamberlain ran down the pike, dimly aware of a roar on either side as his men rose and ran with him through the smoke filling the air.

The shape of a regular rose out of the smoke and Chamberlain's pistol came up and fired as if on its own, the bullet knocking down the regular. There were more regulars in front of him and he fired a second time, then dropped the empty pistol and shifted the sword to his right hand, swinging wildly at another regular, who made a desperate attempt to ward off the blow with his rifle, then dropped the weapon and ran.

Chamberlain staggered, swung at another figure rushing past, then stopped as he became aware that no more regulars were close by. His men were shouting triumphantly, and raising his gaze Chamberlain saw the regulars running, most of them having thrown away their weapons and packs, running back down the Baltimore Pike past the farmhouse and the two cannon still positioned there. A single officer on horseback was trying to rally the regulars, but they streamed past in a panic.

The volunteers kept chasing the regulars, down the slope and onto level ground. Something was wrong, Chamberlain realized. But what? Then he remembered Stuart's cavalry to the north. If the regular cavalry realized what was happening, disengaged from Buford's forces and swept south around the edge of the hills it would catch Chamberlain's men in the open where they would be as helpless as the Roman legions facing the Parthian horsemen at Carrhae. "Hold!" he shouted. "Halt the charge! Back to your positions!"

He probably wouldn't have succeeded in halting the charge except for two things. The regulars' cannon fired, reminding the volunteers that they would have to charge those guns if they kept attacking. But the defenders were also exhausted and stumbling to a halt, lacking the fear which lent speed and strength to the fleeing regular infantry. Gathering together the defenders, Chamberlain led them back up the hill and into their positions, everyone picking up weapons and cartridge boxes abandoned by the regulars. When they were in place once more on top of the hill, the volunteers were well-armed and had plenty of ammunition even though their numbers had been thinned by the fighting.

Chamberlain brought up Armistead's field glasses and looked north, trying to figure out what was happening between the mounted forces in the town. Regular cavalrymen were still swirling around the east edge of the town, small groups dashing in among the buildings, followed by the distant pop of guns firing and gouts of smoke visible from some of the windows, before the regulars fell back again with a few more saddles empty. But, as he watched, Chamberlain saw another horseman ride up from the south, gesturing urgently, and the regular cavalry began forming up and withdrawing to the southeast. "Are they going to come at us?" he wondered aloud.

Sergeant Maines shook his head. "I would think they would be coming right south, straight at us, if that was their intent, sir. Looks more like they're being pulled back to screen the infantry we just sent scurrying. That's what the book says to do, use the cavalry to cover for infantry."

Chamberlain kept his eyes on the regular cavalry, but the sergeant's assessment proved accurate as the horsemen swung wide around the edge of the hills and south toward the Baltimore Pike. "They're not moving very fast."

"The horses are worn out, I expect, sir," Maines suggested. "After all that action they're in no shape for more charges today."

But since Buford's men had fought from cover, their horses would be rested, Chamberlain realized. Over the course of this battle, some important advantages had shifted to the volunteers.

A horseman left the town, riding straight for the hill at a good clip and arriving in a flurry of dust. "Where's Major Armistead?" the rider asked, looking around and saluting quickly.

Chamberlain gestured over toward where Armistead's body lay. "Dead. After we repulsed the first attacks under his command.

I'm Captain Chamberlain." He marveled for a moment how easily that title came to him. In the course of a few hours Professor Chamberlain had gone, replaced by a soldier. "I have been in command since Major Armistead died."

The horseman stared at Chamberlain. "It was you who held the position, sir? And led the charge?"

"Yes. Only after Major Armistead died. He commanded against the first two attacks." It seemed very important to say that, to let everyone know that this had been a battle which Major Armistead had won by his placement of the defenders and effective leadership.

A startled grin spread over the rider's face. "Captain Buford sends his respects, sir, and his congratulations and admiration for your action here." The smile faded. "But a sad loss, sir. The victory was dearly bought." He turned to point toward the town. "Captain Buford wishes to inform you, sir, that he is confident of holding the town until sunset, but believes that enemy reinforcements are on the way and that the enemy may attempt to outflank our current positions in the dark. He recommends falling back under cover of night to meet up beyond the town and be prepared with the dawn to jointly defend that ridge to the west of the town where the Chambersburg Pike passes through. McPherson Ridge it's called. Captain Buford believes that even if the enemy is pressing us, we'll be able to fall back again down the pike to where a gap pierces the next ridge near a place called Herr's Tavern. If we do that, it is Captain Buford's belief that we will have ensured Colonel Hancock's force is safe from our pursuers."

Chamberlain looked around, taking in the land to the north and west. Dust visible along a road in the far distance might well be that raised by Hancock's column and the wagons with it. They had bought enough time that Lincoln had a good chance of escaping, with all that meant for placing a civilian of small means and great purpose at the head of the effort to restore liberty to all, but the price had indeed been very high. "Tell Captain Buford that, uh, Captain Chamberlain sends his respects and, uh, agrees with Captain Buford's proposed course of action." There was something about withdrawals at night that was tugging at Chamberlain's memory, something from his reading. Herodotus, that was it. "Tell him that we will light large watch fires along the ridge before withdrawing, so as to make it appear that we remain occupying this position through the night."

"Excellent, sir." The rider saluted briskly, then tugged his horse around and spurred the stallion back toward the town.

Chamberlain stood watching the rider as Sergeant Maines came up beside him. "Relax if you can, sir," the sergeant advised. "There won't be any more attacks today. It's over."

"Over for today, you mean."

"Aye, sir, I do mean that."

"How many men did we lose?"

"I'll do another muster, but by my last count we've thirty men left on their feet." The sergeant turned to look southeastward. "It will be war now. No more skirmishes in the woods, but our volunteers in stand-up fights against whatever armies the federal government can raise. Both sides raising big armies that'll make this battle look like a skirmish. A war for the Republic. What'll they call it, do you think, sir? The Second American Revolution?"

"Perhaps." Chamberlain looked to the south as well, to where the flags of the US Army fluttered around the artillery which had fallen silent for now. "But we will be fighting for control of the federal government. Both sides will try to control Washington, DC, and ensure the government there reflects their wishes. That would make it a civil war."

"A civil war?" Sergeant Maines spat into the grass. "They'll give Lee command of the whole US Army. You'll see. He'll be the one we have to defeat to get into Washington, but I don't expect he'll just sit behind the forts there and wait for us. Colonel Lee will go on the attack, mark my words." The sergeant pointed toward the town. "I guess they'll name this battle after that place. What's its name?"

"Gettysburg," Chamberlain answered. "Crossroads like this tend to attract battles, and there are likely to be more here, but this one will be remembered. The battle where the war for liberty and the soul of our Republic truly began. It may be a long road, I fear."

"Some roads you got to walk. Some things are worth fighting for."

"Yes, sergeant. Some things are." Chamberlain wondered when he would see his wife and family again, or his brother, and whether he would survive to see the New Republic. "Do you suppose Lincoln will ever come back here? If he will once again look upon this place where men died for the sake of liberty?"

"I've heard him talk," Sergeant Maines offered. "He'd give a fine speech if he came back to Gettysburg. Lincoln would tell everyone why we fought here. And why some died here."

"I hope you are right." Captain Joshua Chamberlain of the Army of the New Republic gestured toward the cemetery gate arch. "We will have to leave Major Armistead's body here when we depart. I will ask the cemetery keeper to inform Colonel Lee when the regulars enter the town. Colonel Lee will see to it that the major's remains are taken care of properly."

"Yes, sir."

"Send some men to get the town doctor to tend our wounded and any wounded regulars in front of our position. They are also to get food and water for everyone. Let the remainder of the men rest. We will have more marching tonight and perhaps more fighting tomorrow." *Tomorrow, and tomorrow, and tomorrow*, the bard's words echoed in Chamberlain's head. But one of those tomorrows would see the New Republic.

Maines grimaced. "Maybe this time we'll make sure the revolution don't get stolen. Something sure went wrong last time."

Chamberlain stared to the east, to where the distant, unseen waters of the Atlantic Ocean rolled, thinking about the British and French warships which patrolled outside of American waters, trying to intercept the slave ships which still sometimes tried to reach American ports. He thought of what Lincoln had said, that slavery had divided the Republic against itself, creating a weakness which those who politicized the US military had exploited, and what Armistead had said, how slave holders too easily accepted the idea of controlling other people as well. "Last time we did not fight to free everyone," Chamberlain said, "and that laid the foundation for bondage for us all. This time it will be different. Someday this will be a free country for all who live here, and this time it will stay free."